—— *Musings of a* ——
Global Nomad

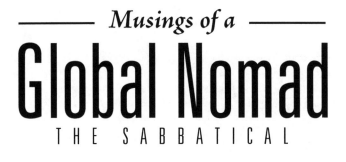

Musings of a
Global Nomad
THE SABBATICAL

R A J A   L A L A

iUniverse LLC
Bloomington

MUSINGS OF A GLOBAL NOMAD
The Sabbatical

This is a work of fiction. All of the characters, names, incidents,
organizations, and dialogue in this novel are either the products
of the author's imagination or are used fictitiously.

iUniverse books may be ordered through booksellers or by contacting:

iUniverse LLC
1663 Liberty Drive
Bloomington, IN 47403
www.iuniverse.com
1-800-Authors (1-800-288-4677)

ISBN: 978-1-4917-2970-0 (sc)
ISBN: 978-1-4917-2972-4 (hc)
ISBN: 978-1-4917-2971-7 (e)

Library of Congress Control Number: 2014905631

Printed in the United States of America.

iUniverse rev. date: 03/25/2014

Contents

The sabbatical begins

"Excuse me; I believe you're in my seat."

Ray looked up, startled and somewhat embarrassed, to see a breathtakingly beautiful young woman standing beside him.

"I was just getting a view of Europe before starting my sabbatical," said Ray with a smile, recovering his composure. He helped her with the cabin baggage and they settled into their assigned seats.

"A sabbatical? So, are you going on a round-the-world-trip too?" she asked.

Ray's thoughts floated back to the past two months which ultimately resulted in this conversation. Due to the economic crisis, Ray's company had offered a voluntary sabbatical to the employees in order to reduce costs. He had seen a lot of the world already, ranging from Japan to Argentina and there were still places he had not yet seen so when the chance came to go on a sabbatical for half a year, he thought, "Why not?"

He had asked his more experienced backpacking friends for advice. His first conversation was with Ellen, a quirky friend who always seemed to be on holidays.

"You should go to compact regions like South East Asia or Central America where it is easy to move from one place to another by road. Also they are quite Visa friendly, so it's easy to cross borders."

As a result, he decided to start his journey in South East Asia and perhaps go to Central America afterwards. He had previously never travelled for such a long time at one go; typically he took vacations for two to three weeks at a time.

Next he met up for coffee with Anouk and Karin, both avid travellers and tall, blond and lissom, as the young ladies in Utrecht (Ray's domicile), often were. Both had been to South East Asia and they sketched out their routes and hidden "gems" of places they had been to. Backpackers seemingly were always on the lookout for places off the beaten track.

"It's beautiful, cheap, the people are very friendly and the food is excellent!"

"Is it difficult to travel alone?" he had asked.

"Not at all, there are so many backpackers travelling alone; it's really quite easy," was the unanimous response.

They gave him advice on practicalities from carrying enough razors to silk-sheets which are light and can be used as a cover or a bed sheet if the sheets in a hostel are dirty. Lastly he met up with his American buddy Jake who gave him all the practical tips for travelling light, from vacuum-bags to head-torches for the nightly jaunt to the shared bathrooms in hostels.

"You're leaving me alone in Utrecht bud," Jake remarked then as he gave Ray a hug.

"Well take care of it for me."

Going to the Dutch travel advice department of the city council had been also an experience in itself; they seemed to conjure up a vaccination for every disease known to man in their advice to Ray. After vacillating for awhile, he had taken all of the recommended vaccines with the thought, "better safe than sorry."

He thereafter had decided to try some dry-runs with a filled backpack on the Catherijne Singel, a small area of green space in the heart of Utrecht where he often went walking. It must have been a funny sight to other users of the pathway as he trekked along with a backpack on the path normally frequented by joggers and walkers. With every walk though, his capacity and endurance had seemed to increase.

The last day at work had been a bit surreal; he had worked right until the last minute before his trip and then handed over his laptop, car and mobile. One of his colleagues had arranged impromptu drinks for which there was a sizable turnout considering it was a last-minute mid-week gig. Ray was the youngest in his team of business development executives. His boss loved giving speeches and that evening was no exception.

"When the sabbatical scheme was launched, I thought of our team and immediately thought that Ray was most likely to apply for it." He paused for effect and added, "After all, the rest of us have wives and kids to look after." He then said, "Actually I am a bit jealous, cheers!"

A colleague offered to drop him home. "Take a lot of photos, I want to re-live all your experiences," said his colleague. "The last time I went backpacking I must have been twenty-one."

Ray laughed and said, "Guess I'll be the quite the old hippie backpacker."

He had had one free day the next day before heading off to Asia and he decided to buy a compact camera, rather than carrying his trusted Single Lens Reflex (SLR) Camera. An SLR did not quite cut the backpacking image plus it was more cumbersome and had a higher chance of getting stolen.

The big day came and Ellen drove him to the airport. He was touched by the gesture. "It's much nicer to start such a long journey with someone dropping you off to the airport," she said.

Ray could not agree more, as he felt a strange lump in his throat. He was going to give up his normal life, friends, family, sports, hobbies and the daily life for the coming half-year and for the first time he felt a bit of trepidation. He gave Ellen a bear-hug and started making his way to the airport gate. The first leg of the journey was from Amsterdam to London and after a quick stopover of a few hours onwards to Bangkok, Thailand.

Ray preferred a window seat on short-haul flights and an aisle one for the long-haul variant, which always seemed to go on forever, and thankfully having accumulated numerous air-miles and a platinum frequent flyer status he usually got his preferred seat. He started reading the Financial Times and could not resist thinking about the financial mess the western world found itself in. Countries living beyond their means and the politics of blandly looking away from the Trojan horses of bloated public sectors and early retirement; tax-evasion and corruption at the cost of prudence. The common man in the besieged countries was feeling the pressure of this anomaly; not the rich and government officials in those countries. He wondered if half a year would be enough for the western world to recover from this crisis.

His reverie was suddenly broken by the sight of a gorgeous girl walking down the aisle. She had a slight tan, long dark hair falling to her shoulders, blue eyes, was about the same height as he and a voluptuous figure. Ray had always had a soft spot for damsels with dark hair and blue eyes.

The aisle seat was still empty and in a reflex reaction he straightened himself and hoped she would take the seat; however, she glided past and carried on walking to the rear of the plane. When passing though, she gave him one of the loveliest smiles he had seen in recent times. He remembered back to a trip to Jaipur, Rajasthan, in India. There he had visited the world famous Amer Fort. The forts guide had led a tour group, Ray included, to a small dark room and then, striking up a match the entire room had suddenly became illuminated due to the hundreds of small mirrors spread all around its surface. The sight of this girls smile had had a similar effect now on Ray, lighting his senses.

"Ah well, probably for the better," he said to himself. "For one thing, this is a short flight to London and secondly; it's not great timing to meet someone when I am going away for a few months."

He had only bought a one-way ticket from London to Bangkok and made a booking in a guest-house for the first few nights, the rest he would figure out on the way. His sister, who lived in London, was going to meet up with him at Heathrow airport as he had not seen her in a number of months.

The flight from Amsterdam to London was as short as usual; the plane took off, reached cruising height and almost immediately began its descent. He had a three hour stopover at Heathrow airport and went through customs (to the land side as it is called) to meet up with his sister, Rina.

She was the older of the two but while their birthdays were just one day apart, both were Pisceans. Pisceans are known for their day-dreaming and artistic abilities and both siblings fit that description. However, they were quite different otherwise in their personalities; Ray was calmer and a bigger risk-taker while Rina was more temperamental and risk-averse. So while Ray changed jobs every four to five years, Rina had been with the same company for almost the entirety of her career.

Ray's family was now spread across the globe, their parents in Delhi, Ray in the Netherlands and Rina in London. Rina had liked to mother Ray since they were kids and Ray was the rebel without a cause. While growing up, the siblings used to quarrel unabated but, funnily enough, when he moved away from home they finally got closer. She worked for an airline and it was due to her airline concession that his first trip to Europe had been possible. The extensive travelling to remote and exotic destinations like Japan and Argentina had also been made easier through her, something for which Ray was always thankful.

Ray saw his sister across the airport before she noticed him. Rina was a pretty woman, and Ray noticed men watching her as she walked briskly to greet him. He was glad to see she had a big smile and that she was in good spirits.

"I've thought it through and it's a great idea that you're going on a sabbatical to explore the world!" she said greeting him.

"Well, not exactly the world, but yeah it's great! I was curious, you seemed a bit apprehensive when we first talked about it, at least that was my impression; so what made you change your mind?" inquired Ray.

"I think we should all take more risks and explore the possibilities of life," said Rina. "Besides which, you're single and fancy-free, with no mouths to feed, so it's good that you're taking the plunge."

Rina presented him the Lonely Planet guide to South-East Asia, thoughtful as ever. It was aptly titled "On a Shoestring"; this was after all the first backpacking adventure for Ray.

"Thanks dear! Great reading for the long flight ahead to Bangkok."

She treated Ray to lunch at the airport during which Ray started to get in the holiday mood. "How heavy is your backpack?" she inquired.

"It's about thirteen kilo's. Pretty light eh?" Ray replied with a winning smile.

Rina, suddenly sounding anxious, said, "Our parents are still a bit worried you know? Of course you are an experienced traveller but you've never backpacked before."

Ray looked to reassure her, "True, that's why I've done some preparation. It seemed that everyone I asked had a story to tell, the optimistic ones usually told a fabulous story, whilst others would give me tales of horror and woe, of how their stuff was stolen or of corrupt officials and the like."

He paused and added, "The thing is, I think you always find what you seek. Those seeking an adventure and new exciting experiences are more likely to find that whereas those afraid of getting into trouble are most likely to find exactly that."

The remaining time passed quickly; and so he bid her farewell, boarded the flight, took the window seat and mused about the past period which had flown by so quickly.

"Excuse me, I believe you're in my seat," he heard a feminine voice saying. Lost in his thoughts, he had taken the window seat instead of the aisle, as was his preference on the long-flights.

He looked up, startled and somewhat embarrassed, and saw the same breathtakingly beautiful girl from the flight from the Amsterdam to London flight . . .

✦

Ray mentally returned to the present to continue his conversation with the lovely damsel. "Not entirely a round the world trip but a mini one to South East Asia, for three-four months, then I head back home, thereafter perhaps to Central America. What about you?"

"I'm also starting out in South East Asia, then heading to Australia and New Zealand, before moving on to South and Central America and, if I have money left that is, to Africa before returning back home to the Netherlands," she said.

She paused and added, "I am Dutch, by the way."

"Oh I know," said Ray.

"Really, how come?"

"Well, I saw you on the flight from Amsterdam."

"Ah, I thought it was my accent. You aren't Dutch, are you? I would think Latin, no?"

"Well, kind of Dutch, at least that what my passport says, though I grew up in India. Trouwens, ik spreek ook Nederlands hoor[1]," said Ray.

"You have a cute accent. I think though that it's better for me to practice my English. I always pictured Indians with big moustaches, like the one you see in films. How did you end up in cold Netherlands of all places?"

"Well, funnily enough I never had plans of living abroad whilst growing up. That all changed though when I first came to Europe on vacation . . ."

"Ah let me guess, ten countries in three weeks like all the other tourists."

"Actually no, I came with my family, we selected a few cities, London, Paris, Amsterdam and in and around Oberhausen, as we have an offshoot of the family in Germany. We spent around four days in every city on average."

". . . And after that you decided to stay in Amsterdam?" she said.

"Well not exactly, since I am from outside the EU, the procedure was pretty complicated. When I went back to India, I thought it

---

[1]   I also speak Dutch

would be a great idea to work and travel in Europe for a few years before going to the US, do an MBA and become an investment banker."

"So you are not a slum dog millionaire?" she said whilst laughed out loud.

"What is it with everyone and stereotypes?"

"Oh I'm sorry! I was just kidding really . . . . so do you feel more Dutch or Indian now?" Daphne replied looking slightly abashed.

"Well, I like to think of myself as a Global Nomad, belonging everywhere in general and nowhere in particular. I quite like the work-life balance in the Netherlands and I have a lot of hobbies, that's probably why I've lingered so long."

"What are your hobbies then?"

"The past few years, I've developed my artistic side. Initially salsa dancing, thereafter photography and painting; and I even acted in a small musical production last year," he smiled and inquired, "What's your story?"

"Very boring in comparison, I am Dutch and was born and brought up in Amsterdam. I studied in Utrecht, Communications Management and have now been working in that field for a couple of years. Anyway, I was made redundant in my last role, so am going on a world trip with the severance payment I got."

"What a coincidence, I live in Utrecht."

"Really? Whereabouts?"

"In the centre of course! I love Utrecht; prefer it to Amsterdam for living, though I work in Amsterdam."

"Oh, I thought most foreigners liked Amsterdam."

"Well, most tourists like Amsterdam, whereas most expats like Rotterdam, which has more of a city feeling to it, however I like Utrecht."

"What do you like so much about it?"

"It's got a compact centre, the lovely feel of Old Dutch cities with its canals and a very well preserved city-centre. Did you know that it was in the list of Lonely Planet's Top Ten of the world's unsung places?"

"Oh really, I expect it'll be full of hordes of tourists soon! What do you like the most?"

"Hmm, I love walking around the centre, discovering the small alleys and corridors, of course there are the very picturesque canals like the Oudegracht with old houses lining them. Actually, I have some photos with me on Camera, have a look."

Oudegracht

He continued, "I also love the view from La Place restaurant; Utrecht looks like an old medieval city from an aerial view."

View of Utrecht centre from La Place

"Wow, these are nice photos," she exclaimed. "I live, or rather used to live, in the Centre also, in a small student room in Hamburgerstraat."

"That's close to where I live. So we were almost neighbours, and never met I am Ray, by the way."

"I am Daphne, pleased to meet you," she said while stretching out a hand.

"Enchanté."

"So you also speak French?"

"Je me débrouille si je suis en vacance en France,"[2] Ray said with a smile.

"Hablo espagnol,"[3] Daphne responded in competition.

"Yo tambien, pero un poco básico."[4]

"Show off! Are you trying to impress me?"

"Well, are you impressed?"

"A bit."

"Then I'll say I speak six languages."

---

[2]   I manage if I am on vacations in France

[3]   I speak Spanish

[4]   Me too, but a bit basic

"Holy cow, I am such an underachiever with my three," she said with a smile and rolling her eyes. "So, did you learn them to impress women?"

"Of course, why else?"

She giggled and said, "Well, I'm the wrong woman you're trying to impress, as I just broke up with my boyfriend and I'm not really looking for anything new right now. Plus of course I am gonna be travelling the world . . ."

"Pretty much straight to the point eh?"

"We Dutch are known for that," she said shrugging her shoulders and then asked, "What about you, looking to find your love on your sabbatical?"

Ray smiled and said, "Not really. I am what they call a late bloomer."

"Ah, what's the story there then?"

"Well, in my twenties I felt probably a bit young to settle down. When I moved to the Netherlands, I had originally moved to Eindhoven. I think I exuded an exotic foreign air and coupled with my accent, got involved in several passionate but short relationships . . ."

"Eindhoven of all places to arrive! It's such an industrial city."

"Yes, of all places. Well Eindhoven was a nice and well-kept city and it was anyways exotic to be in a different country. After a few years however, I felt the urge to move to a more bustling city and moved to Utrecht."

". . . and there you met your lady-love?" asked Daphne.

"Umm, sort of. I got into a relationship with someone who was nine years younger and nine centimetres taller," he smiled and added, "However we were in different phases of life, she was still a student and anyhow after about two years we broke up. Then I started an executive MBA, but next to my full-time job I had little time for romancing. Now I am done, in my mid thirties with a twin desire; on the one hand I want to settle down and have a family; on the other hand I want to be independent and travel the world. Perhaps we could combine that and do it together?" he concluded with a wink.

"Whoa man, you too get straight to the point eh?"

"Well, I've become as direct as my Dutch passport would encourage me to be."

"Umm, I am afraid you'll have to look further."

A bit stumped, Ray looked around reflectively and smiled broadly at the air-hostess passing by. She leaned over and inquired if he was having a nice flight. He responded with a twinkle, "I am thanks; especially when there are such nice cabin-crew personnel onboard."

"A bit of a player, aren't you?" teased Daphne when she had left.

Ray laughed and said, "A player and a gentleman, as a dear friend of mine recently remarked. I have traits of both and in a given situation one of the two prevails over the other."

"So, what role are you playing with me?"

"A gentleman of course."

"So, time will tell?"

"Yes," said Ray, unable to stifle an unintentional yawn.

"That boring, am I?"

"Yes," he said it with a wink, "and I haven't slept much, I was so excited about the trip."

"You should get your beauty sleep then."

"Good idea. Talk to you later dear."

He dozed off, aware that the rapport was building up well with his new acquaintance. Ray had never been very perceptive of women's interest in him. He was always apprehensive that if he misread the interest he would make a big fool of himself. So, it was his defence mechanism to treat most initial contact with new women as friendly.

He awoke to the aroma of food being served and looked up groggily at Daphne, who seemed to be looking at him curiously.

"I really have to go to the washroom and I was hoping you would wake up soon, but I didn't want to wake you as you were sleeping so peacefully," she said softly, in response to Ray's inquiring look.

"So what are your plans in Thailand?" he asked when she had returned.

"I'll spend a few days in Bangkok and then go to the Islands in the South, where I am going to live the beach-life for a long, long time, go to some full-moon parties and probably do some yoga and go to a health resort. And you?"

"I have a booking for the first couple of nights in Bangkok at a guest-house called Shanti Lodge near Khaosan road, that's all I have really planned at the moment. I'll probably go up North to Chiang Mai, meet up with a friend who lives there and then head south too. Then onwards to Cambodia and Vietnam, trying to live the unplanned experience . . . Do you have a hostel booked in Bangkok?"

"Nope. I am going to find a place on Khaosan road; it's the place to be for backpackers. Where's your guest-house?"

"It's near the river and I believe its fifteen minutes by foot to Khaosan. We could meet up perhaps?"

"Sure. I don't have a local mobile number yet, but you could find me on Facebook, Daphne Dijkstra."

"Perfect, I'll find you!"

The rest of the flight passed quickly, with the pleasure of nice company accompanied by small-talk and before he knew it, the plane touched down at Svarnabhumi airport in Bangkok. Ray remarked that that was a Sanskrit name meaning Golden land.

Backpacks collected from the baggage belt and a quite seamless pass-through immigration later, they took the airport rail-link which took passengers to the city, cheaply and quickly. While on the train looking out of the window, Ray got an unmistakable impression of Asia. High rises next to slums, lots of traffic on small bikes, he was sure he would smell delicious food as soon as he stepped outside. However as they stepped out at the Phaya Thai station they were confronted instead with hot and humid air and the smell of heavy traffic.

"Wow, what a contrast to Europe!" Ray said with look of discomfort on his face.

"Yeah, I love it," was Daphne's reply.

They made their way down to the road where they had to find a taxi or a tuk-tuk to take them to their different destinations.

Daphne wanted to try a tuk-tuk immediately so when they hailed down one, Ray offered it to her.

"Thanks gentleman," she said and after a pause she continued, "I was so sure you would make a move on me."

Having said that, she gave him a small kiss on the lips and was off before he could react.

"Until tomorrow? Or the day after?" shouted Ray trying to subdue the traffic noise.

Daphne gestured with her hands, circling around her ears, that she could not hear him and with that she was gone with the wind.

So began Ray's journey in Thailand . . .

Sawadee Khrap

Ray took a taxi to Shanti Lodge and was surprised that the price by meter was less than the price the tuk-tuk driver had offered. "Mental note to self, always take a metered taxi."

The Shanti Lodge was just like the guide book had described it, Shanti means peace in Sanskrit. It was a small cosy and tranquil guesthouse in one of the many tiny bustling streets of Bangkok. This neighbourhood did smell like the Asia Ray had hoped for, the distinct smell of lemongrass and fresh herbs filled the air.

After unpacking his bags and a shower, Ray went to the restaurant part of the guest house and sat down for dinner. The décor was simple and tasteful; massive wood tables of different shapes arranged in a non-linear fashion and lined by chairs of various shapes and rocking benches. 'How different from Europe where the accent is on everything being symmetric,' thought Ray.

"Are you eating alone?" said a genial looking bloke as he sat down in the facing chair. He had a short cropped haircut, was broad set and of muscular built and looked like he had come straight from the army.

"Yeah, just arrived in town," said Ray.

"The name's Tom, welcome to Bangkok dude!"

"I am Ray, pleased to meet you. Been here long?"

"Yeah man, about a week already, just graduated from high-school back in the States, gonna chill and explore this country before I join the service."

'Hmm, I'll be the oldie in these circles,' thought Ray. "Been in Bangkok all this while?" he inquired.

"Yeah mate, been hanging here, the staff here take good care of me," said Tom waving his hand in the general direction of the personnel.

"Sawadee kha," greeted one of the waiting staff. "Would you like to order?"

Ray ordered a green-curry, a perennial favourite.

Tom ordered a stir-fry and added, "The food is extremely good here; I eat the other meals of the day on the street-side to save money for dinner here. It's always crowded in the weekends with expats."

Looking around, Ray noticed expat-looking people at the other tables in somewhat more formal attire and others in travel gear, probably backpackers who were lodging at the guest-house.

Tom continued, "So what are your plans here?"

"Well, I am going to hit the temples tomorrow; meet a friend in the evening and thereafter I don't know," said Ray, smiling as he thought of Daphne. "Which reminds me, any internet cafes around here?"

"Yeah, one around the corner," said Tom. "I haven't done a lot of sightseeing yet, just chilling and loads of partying."

The food arrived and the green curry was simply delicious, the Dutch expression for which would be, 'It was as if an angel was pissing on your tongue.' 'The Dutch are a funny lot,' thought Ray, as he devoured his food. The ingredients were fresh, the curry sharp and the rice sticky.

"Well mate, I am pretty jet-lagged, and I have to send a few messages from the internet café and then hit the sack," said Ray once the post-dinner dip had kicked in.

"You could use my netbook if it's brief," said Tom jovially.

It struck Ray that the general countenance was quite friendly, he wondered if the entire backpacking experience would be similar— like being part of a big family of travellers. He was beginning to enjoy the experience and said, "That would be great."

Ray wrote a short email to all his well-wishers still at home and then looked up Daphne on Facebook. He found her and wrote about meeting the next evening at eight-ish, half wondering whether the meeting would happen.

"Hoi Tom," shouted another jovial-looking bloke with a beard and a sizable beer belly as he entered the guest house. Ray was a big fan of the comic strip Tintin and this bloke reminded Ray of a jovial version of Captain Haddock.

"Heya Jan!" said Tom to the genial bloke.

"My friend arrived from Belgium today; this is Anne-Cecile," said Jan introducing a cute and dainty looking brunette, quite petite in stature.

Anne-Cecile said, "Nice to meet you," she said as she stretched her artistic looking hands.

"I am Ray, enchanté. Komen jullie uit Vlanderen?⁵"

"Ik ben Jan en inderdaad Vlaams, AC is from Wallonie⁶; so her Dutch is very poor," Jan said with a wink.

"Yes indeed, friends call me AC," said Anne-Cecile.

Anne-Cecile and Jan sat down and ordered some beers. Ray decided to stay a bit longer for a drink with the friendly group.

"So, where are you from? How long have you been here?" Jan asked Ray.

This was going to be an oft-repeated conversation among backpackers . . .

"I'm Indian, live in the Netherlands and just started my backpacking tour. Where in Belgium do you live?"

"Brugge," said Jan and A.C. in unison.

A couple of drinks and pleasantries later, they all decided to explore Bangkok together the next day. Ray was exhausted but happy with his first day of travelling. He had a private single room on the first floor, but the bathrooms and toilet were shared.

He woke up fresh the next day; and though he was normally a light sleeper in new surroundings, the past night he had slept like a baby. He came out straightaway for breakfast to the restaurant area.

"Sawadee kha," he said to the girl on duty. He had practised some basic phrases the previous night.

---

5   Translates to "Are you from Vlanderen?" (The Flemish part of Belgium)
6   I am Jan and indeed Flemish, AC is from Wallonie. Belgium has a Flemish speaking part and a French one, the latter called Wallonie.

She giggled and said, "That is for a woman"

"Oh, so what must a man say? Could you write for me?"

'Sawadee Khrap,' she wrote on her note-pad and handed it to him.

Looking at the menu and feeling his growling stomach he ordered the extended breakfast, which was approximately the same price as one coffee back home and sat down with the Bangkok Post. There was no sign of the others yet. The breakfast arrived, consisting of toast, omelette, hash browns, fried tomatoes, yogurt, fresh juice and a cup of coffee. The sun was already shining bright and he enjoyed the ambience on the veranda of Shanti Lodge of street hawkers, schoolchildren neatly dressed in uniform being heralded by their mothers, and people from all walks of life on the busy street. In the distance he could see a shining temple. The others came in just as he finished breakfast.

"I'll shower and get ready while you guys have breakfast."

Half an hour later, they were on their way, on a tuk-tuk to the Grand Palace. Ray was getting the hang of the system. The price had to be negotiated in advance and it had to be reasonable. If the driver was quoting too low, one was probably being taken for a ride, literally and figuratively, to shops and markets rather than the destination one wanted to go to.

This ride was an experience as the driver weaved his way through traffic at a pace beyond the seemingly permissible, sometimes swerving to the opposite incoming traffic to overtake and returning to the right lane just in time.

Both Anne-Cecile and Ray heaved a sigh of relief when they alighted while the other two laughed at them. They were rewarded with the glorious sight of the temple of the Emerald Buddha looming in the distance. As they made their way towards it, they were confronted by touts who proudly proclaimed, "Palace close today. Come, I take you to sight-seeing Bangkok."

"But I can see people going in there . . ." said Anne-Cecile warily pointing her finger inside the compound.

"Just ignore and walk through," said Jan who was well aware of this common scam.

"This must be the silliest of scam techniques I've seen!" said A.C.

They were early and dressed appropriately, with clothes that covered the shoulders and knees, so they passed through the controls quickly after paying for the entrance tickets.

On entry, the first compound was filled with gleaming stupas, each bearing shining golden leaves. The supporting pillars wore intricate mosaics, the doors were coloured in red and blue and the pediments made of marble.

Temple complex

Saffron coloured robe-clad monks streamed in and out of the compound completing the ambience of majestic serenity. This temple was considered one of the holiest by the Thais and therefore heavily visited. No photos were allowed in the main complex and they had to sit with folded knees, in any case not to point at the Buddha. The Emerald Buddha statue was incidentally made of the material Jasper and not of emerald as its name suggested.

The atmosphere was quite intense as local Thais from all walks of life offered their prayers. Ray was a Hindu albeit not a very religious one and not into organized religious forms. He however absorbed the intensity of the surrounding people and performed a small prayer. They then went for a view of the adjoining Grand palace. The grounds were vast, the walls of the building were white; a nice contrast to the golden stupas. The roofs were very ornate like the stupas. They wandered around for a couple of hours, soaking in the ambience and quietude of the vast grounds in the middle of bustling Bangkok.

"Look, there's a miniature of Angkor Wat, one of the places I want to go to in Cambodia," said Anne-Cecile as they made their way back towards the exit.

"I'll plan to go there in the coming months," said Ray.

Once outside, they wanted to take a tuk-tuk to the nearby Wat Pho, which housed the biggest reclining Buddha in the country and the usual haggling started.

"Do you work here?" one of the cab-drivers inquired Ray.

Ray instinctively said yes and the driver agreed to go with the meter.

'He probably thought I was a Buddhist,' mused Ray due to the fact that he shaved his head regularly since a few years; a clean head looked better than his receding hairline.

All through his travels, people were always confused with Ray's origin which was a distinct advantage, as the locals thought him to be one of them but perhaps of mixed blood or settled elsewhere. When dancing Salsa back home in the Netherlands, Latinos would sometimes come up to him and start speaking Spanish to him, thinking he was of Latin blood.

The taxi stopped after just a couple of minutes at their destination, Wat Pho, which was the oldest temple in Bangkok. This temple was much quieter than the temple of the Emerald Buddha, having fewer hordes of tourists. Once inside, they were confronted with the country's largest reclining Buddha, in full golden glory.

"Quite bling eh?" remarked Tom.

Afterwards, the troupe decided to go to Jim Thompson's house, which had been converted into a local museum. Thompson had been an American entrepreneur, who was initially in Thailand for the US military, who after quitting service settled down in Bangkok and became involved in the Thai silk business. He collected art from all over Thailand and the house in which he lived had since been converted into a museum and preserved as an example of how the rich lived in Bangkok in the fifties and sixties.

Ray thought it was quite interesting, as it gave him insight to the social system prevalent in those days.

Exiting the Thompson house, they realised they were close to the shopping district of Siam Square, so they decided to go there.

Siam Square was very reminiscent of the shopping districts of the rising Asian powers, high-rise malls lining the sky and stocking the luxury brands from Hermes to Cartier. Affluent Thais and foreigners lined up the spaces. At the Siam Paragon there was an IMAX theatre.

"I've never been to an IMAX film, could we go there tomorrow?" asked Anne-Cecile.

Ray agreed and said, "Sounds like a good plan!"

"Shall we go this evening to Khaosan Road to party?" asked Tom.

"Well, I am meeting a girl I met on the plane. I need to check my email to know the time and place. Perhaps we could join you later."

"Ooh, how romantic!" said the boys, rolling their eyes whilst Anne-Cecile smiled.

After sauntering around the malls, Ray found an internet café. He ducked in there quickly whilst the others did some window-shopping. Sure enough, there was a note from Daphne suggesting to meet at eight p.m. at a café called Mulligan's on Khaosan road.

"I've made an appointment for dinner on Khaosan," Ray said as he re-joined the group.

"We could meet at midnight at The Club," suggested Tom.

"Sure! Is there a club called The Club there?"

"Yes, actually there is."

The next stop in their travel was the Grand Palace, which they could only see from far as it was closed for tourists at that moment.

Grand Palace

They made their back to the quiet of Shanti Lodge. Wandering all day in the humid and warm weather had taken its toll and they all went to have a siesta, except Tom who was still full of youthful energy.

After the siesta and getting refreshed, Ray made his way to Khaosan road, which was a relatively small street. It somehow had become famous among backpackers and was now an essential destination on the backpacking route. Ray's first impression was a mix of blaring music, food stalls and neon lights flashing from cheap lodgings. He was glad that he had chosen the laid back Shanti Lodge as his first hostel and not some cramped accommodation at Khaosan.

He made his way to Mulligan's and true to Dutch punctuality; Daphne was waiting outside the café, looking as radiant as ever. She gave him a bear hug.

"Shall we sit outside?" suggested Daphne.

"Good plan."

They took a place at the restaurant on the opposite side of Mulligan's.

"So, how have you been? How's the backpacking life treating you, are you enjoying it?" asked Daphne.

"I did sightseeing for the most part today, with some other backpackers I met back in the Shanti Lodge. The backpacker life is great, people are friendly and laidback; it seems like a big family."

"What is actually the reason that you are backpacking; I mean are you trying to find yourself?"

Ray smiled and said, "Not really, I don't think I need to go thousands of kilometres away from daily life to find myself. He paused to think and added, "I don't know, I got a chance to travel and I took it. Now that you ask though; all through the years I've heard people go gaga over backpacking on a world-trip, so now I am intrigued to know what it is about. What's it to you then?"

"Hmm, I want to discover more of myself by taking a break from regular life plus I love to travel and meet people."

"Well, that goes for me too. I actually have no expectations in particular; let's see where this takes me . . . So how was your day?"

"Well, I slept in, got a Thai massage, did a bit of sightseeing and then booked a ticket southwards to the Islands. I am going to Ko Samui tomorrow."

Ray was taken aback and expressed a muttered, "Oh?"

"Yes, I want to hit the beaches and I anyway have to fly out of Bangkok, so I'll see it when I am back."

"I could come down south too," said Ray hopefully.

"Oh, you are such a cutie and I like you much more than I wanted to," she trailed and then added rapidly, "The thing is, I've just come out of a difficult long distance relationship and am not really ready for something new. Plus I don't want to do that long-distance thing again and I will probably be away for a year."

"I understand," said Ray gravely.

"Oh, don't look so disappointed. We could make this a night to remember."

"True."

A 'night to remember' it became, after downing a couple of beers; Daphne suggested a spicy street-food joint. It was an authentic, extremely hot stir-fry and Ray felt the fresh chillies inflaming his mouth.

"Mmm lekker[7]," Daphne said while shaking her right hand to and fro besides her ears. It was a Dutch gesture, the Indian equivalent being joining the index finger and thumb in a small semi-circle.

"Ya lekker," said Ray bravely trying to be manly but the sweat broke out on his shaved head; at the sight of which Daphne started laughing loud.

"Are you laughing at me?"

She laughed and said, "Well yes. I would have thought that you could deal with even hotter food."

"Well, I've lost the skill after so many years of living in Europe."

"Ah, my best friend is Indonesian, so I've had a lot of Sambal[8] practice."

After cooling down the chillies with chilled beer they hit the dance floor at The Club, which featured techno-music and Ibiza-like ambience. Ray spotted Tom in the distance who was with some local girls.

"Is this your bird?" said Tom into Ray's ear as he came up to talk above the din of the music.

"Daphne, Tom," shouted Ray introducing them and they shook hands.

Ray resumed talking to Tom, "Well, yes and no. She's indeed the one I'd met on the plane, but she's leaving tomorrow."

"Pity, she looks very cute. But man, she's slightly taller than you!"

"Ah, I've become immune to that especially since my previous girlfriend was very tall. Dutch girls are very tall! Where are the Belgians by the way?"

"They went off to sleep. We've arranged to meet in the afternoon to go to the IMAX. Anyways mate, I won't keep you anymore, got my own birds to attend to. See you around," said Tom as he made his way back to the middle of the dance floor.

Daphne and Ray danced together till the wee hours and then parted with a long goodbye kiss.

---

[7]   Meaning delicious
[8]   Spicy paste made from red peppers

And then she was gone . . .

$$+$$

Ray woke up the next day feeling quite dehydrated, an effect of the alcohol from the night before. He had mixed feelings about Daphne; while he realized that it was pretty inconvenient to start something with someone when travelling for the next couple of months, he also knew that it was not often that he met someone whom he really had a click with.

It was almost midday by now and he resolved not to party too much during this sabbatical, as he wanted to make the most of the experience rather than spend half his days in bed. A shower later, he had his usual grand breakfast and was joined by Tom, who had just returned from his morning saunter. Tom could evidently still handle partying till the wee-hours and sleeping marginally.

"What time did you agree to meet Jan and Anne-Cecile?" asked Ray.

"About midday, so they should be here any moment."

"Ok, I'll go and check out the local temple in the meantime."

To reach the local temple, Ray had to pass through the market which smelled mostly of not so fragrant fish, so he held his breath and passed through quickly. This temple was also in a similar style as the others they had seen the previous day but did not have the multitude of tourists swarming the compound.

The Belgians had arrived by the time Ray returned to the Shanti Lodge.

"Hoihoi, where have you been today?" asked Ray.

"Ah, we took the river ferry down to the farthest point, it's very nice, no traffic jams and you can see Bangkok from the river. The stop is quite close from here."

Ray made a mental note to take the ferry some other time. They were ready to go to the IMAX show and by this stage, Ray was getting quite adept in negotiating with taxis, so minutes later, the foursome were on their way to Siam Square on a metered taxi.

The cinema complex was swarming with teenagers out for a date or just hanging out with friends. The only film on the IMAX was 'Real Steel', so they went for it. They took their places in a sparsely populated hall.

Suddenly everybody stood up and the foursome looked at each other in mutual incomprehension but decided to stand up anyway. The reason became clear soon enough—a short video of the King of Thailand engaging in philanthropic activities and everyone watching it in silence.

The film itself was entertaining, though probably the highlight was the IMAX experience and not the storyline. It was getting dark by the time they came out of the theatre.

"Let's go to Patpong market to eat and shop," suggested Tom.

"Pourquoi pas,"[9] said Ray

Patpong was a raunchy place, full of shops selling fake merchandise and yet other places specializing in risqué ping-pong shows for tourists. The street was lined with restaurants and they picked a random one and ordered some food and drinks.

". . . Ping pong show, ping pong show"; "you want Lolex?" were the chants of diverse touts and tradesmen as they ate their Pad Thais and stir fries.

The first shouts caught Ray's attention because he played table tennis at home.

"You find me an opponent and I'll give you a ping pong demonstration," said Ray mischievously whilst performing a shadow top-spin drive to one of the touts who had been pestering them for awhile. The tout gave a bewildered look and left them quickly.

"Say, how did your rendezvous with the girl from the flight go?" asked Anne-Cecile curiously.

"They kissed for about ten minutes," piped in Tom helpfully.

Ignoring Tom's pouted lip-impression, Ray said, "Yes, that was the last I have seen of her. She left for the Islands this evening, probably about now."

"Sad? Disappointed?"

---

9   French phrase meaning "Why not?"

"Not entirely, I think people come and go in your lives . . . plus if it's destined, we'll meet again," said Ray sanguinely, but thought to himself about how much he would have liked to have gone with her.

"Yes, well, we should meet up when you are back in Europe! After all Brugge is not so far from Utrecht."

"And we will."

Tom wanted to buy an imitation watch, so they went looking. The negotiation with the diverse vendors was an adventure in itself, they all had their own negotiating techniques; Tom would look incredulously and say "Oh my God"; Jan would give a snort and quoted half the price in return; Anne-Cecile smiled lovingly and said, "I don't have so much money." In the end the A.C technique was the most successful and Tom got a shiny Tag Heuer look-alike.

"Looks like the real thing!" said Ray with a wink.

"Yeah right," said Tom.

"Excellent last night in Bangkok!" remarked Anne-Cecile.

"Oh, you're leaving too?" Ray was a bit disappointed.

"Yeah, we're going to Ko Tao to go diving with some friends."

"Nice!" said Tom.

"You know guys, I'll leave Bangkok tomorrow too," said Ray coming to a decision.

"Coming to the Islands too?" said A.C.

"Nah, I'll do the opposite, go up north, first probably a night's stay in Ayutthaya, and then up to Chiang Mai to visit my friend." Ray had done some more reading up of the Lonely Planet.

"I'm gonna be left all alone," said Tom with a pout on his face.

"You'll have the local girls to keep you company," said Jan.

Tom gave his usual mischievous grin and said, "Yeah, I'll go to the Islands in a few days though, we should keep in touch."

A.C. said, "It's a small world after all."

And so the little group parted ways . . .

North bound by northern line

T he next morning Ray got his first Thai massage ever. He had previously had Chinese and Shiatsu massages, but this was entirely a different cup of tea. A Thai massage was relatively quite firm; the masseuse used her knuckles and cracked and stretched all of his body. Usually Ray would dose off during a Chinese massage, but for this one he was wide—and painfully awake. The massage must have done him good though, as afterwards he fell into a deep slumber.

He repacked his backpack neatly with his clothes in the vacuum seal bags, checked out before midday and hailed a cab to go to the main train station, Hualamphong. On the busy Bangkok roads to the station, he reflected that the past few days had flown by. While this would be his normal routine for the many city trips he did, he realized that keeping up this tempo for months of travelling would probably be too much of a good thing. Though he did not know exactly what he wanted out of this trip in particular, he at least knew now that he did not want to be a "been there, seen it, done it" backpacker.

The train station was relatively clean and organized and even had a food court on the first floor. There were also some offices of travel companies and Ray went into one of them to assess his future travel plans.

Bangkok was where the trains changed, so he could go up north or down south, but there was not a possibility to go from Chiang Mai in the north direct to the islands down South. The agents were trying to sell flights to Phuket, special offers for the Christmas holidays.

Ray, on hearing this information, formed a route in his mind, to explore north Thailand, perhaps fly directly to Phuket from there, explore the Islands and come back to Bangkok to continue onwards to Cambodia in the New Year. Flying from the North to South Thailand would be more expensive than the night train or bus, but it would save more than a day, plus a lot of extra hassle. With this plan, he went to the train counter to get his tickets to the North.

The woman at the counter spoke little English, but by this time Ray was getting a feel of broken Thai English.

"I go Ayutthaya today and Chiang Mai night train tomorrow. Possible?"

"Ayu-tha-ya?"

"Yes, yes."

"Ok. Local train?"

"Ok."

"Night train Ayutthaya-Chiang Mai, sleep?"

"Yes sleeper. Tomorrow."

"Okay okay."

He got his tickets. The train fare to Ayutthaya was fifteen Baht and the journey was supposedly a two hour ride. It was cheaper than taking a tuk-tuk in Bangkok!

The next train was leaving shortly, so Ray half ran to board it. He took a place on the local train, the seats were quite rickety. An old woman carrying a brood of chickens came to sit next to him. The smell of the woman and the smell of her chicken were almost indistinguishable.

"Sawadee khrap," he said.

"Sawadee ka. Where you from?"

"India, live in Holland."

She pretended to understand, smiled showing her teeth and nodded vigorously as the rickety train jerked to a start.

Ray was the only foreigner in the compartment, so somewhat of a novelty. Soon the locals converged on him and started conversing. The verbal part of the conversation was somewhat limited, however that was pretty much compensated by the non-verbal communication.

"You very handsome," decided the old woman suddenly.

Ray thanked her and wondered how the word had got into her vocabulary.

"You very beautiful," he said.

She flashed her teeth widely. The rickety train made its way across the lush countryside and a couple of hours later reached Ayutthaya. Recent floods had washed away the platform; all that remained were some tracks and pieces of wood where the platform had been. Ray jumped with his backpack and landed on the soft ground, just about managing to keep his balance. His shoes and jeans were covered in mud and he was beginning to see how backpackers got their raggedy appearance.

Ayutthaya, the name based on the name of Indian mythological King Ram's capital Ayodhya. It was the old capital of Siam before the Burmese King plundered it and the Siamese moved on to what is now the present-day Bangkok. From a distance, south-east Asia had seemed to Ray like one homogenous region, but now he was beginning to get a feel for the diversity. It was just like Indians and/ or Europeans seem similar from afar and quite different from near with different food habits, cultures and in-fighting.

"Hello, hello, you want tuk-tuk?" inquired a driver as he zipped his vehicle next to Ray. For a while Ray had been transported into the laid-back countryside, but with a jolt he was back in tuk-tuk land. As a reflex, he did his best manoeuvre, smiling, enclosing his hands in the Namaste form and bowing slightly. Drivers seemed to think he was a travelling monk and when he did the namaste they would leave him alone. The driver drove away.

'It wasn't the smartest thing to do,' Ray realised, as he still had to get into town.

And then . . . he suddenly beheld the sight of 'The backpacker'. This was the quintessential backpacker Ray had pictured while still back home in the Netherlands. He had long braids with beads scattered throughout, a beard in which sparrows could contemplate setting up nest, insects buzzing around the clothes, which looked like they had not been washed since the previous year and the general countenance of a man at peace with the world.

"Wanna share a tuk-tuk?" the venerable backpacker asked, gesturing with his hand in the general direction of the tuk-tuks. He looked like he had been on the road for a while.

"Sure."

The backpacker boarded the tuk-tuk replete with little plastic bags and shoes hanging from an enormous backpack.

"Been a few years on the road?" inquired Ray as he took his place.

"About two months."

"Wow, you look, um well-travelled."

"I was in the jungles of Borneo these two months, now getting back into civilization. I am meeting up with a friend who's here in Ayutthaya."

"Ah, that explains the beard."

"Yeah, I haven't shaved in the past months."

The ride was short and Ray got off at Ayutthaya Guesthouse, which was on the main road. Business was quite slow this year, as the region had been heavily hit by floods and most foreign tourists had kept away, warned by their respective governments. He got a spacious room with an attached bath for a cheaper price than the shared room in Bangkok. Somehow, he was feeling upbeat; he was really on the road now. The hotel owner also sold food in a makeshift restaurant and Ray was hungry by this time so asked for a Pad-Thai.

While eating, a garrulous tuk-tuk driver approached him and started a conversation and then offered him a deal to take around all the sites in Ayutthaya. Ray said he would eat first and think about it. He looked up his Lonely Planet and the sites to visit and agreed on a deal. After all, business was slow here, he considered and the tuk-tuk driver was very friendly.

Ayutthaya was a UNESCO Heritage site and was built at the confluence of three rivers. It had therefore been heavily hit by the recent floods with the water level rising enormously. The hotel owner showed a photo from a few weeks back which showed, covered in water, the very place where Ray now sat enjoying his meal. The road was under water till about the first floor of the hotel and the owner figured on a boat in the photo.

Historic temples and monuments were scattered all over the city and Ray spent the next few hours exploring quite a few of them. He could not but feel a bit sad that this once magnificent city has fallen into ruin when it was sacked by the Burmese.

Some of the ruins still felt the effects of the floods and Ray had to manoeuvre his way across the mud on the ground. His hiking training in the month preceding the sabbatical held him in good stead, as he briskly climbed the stairs of the Wat Phra Si Sanphet with three distinctive bell-shaped towers. There was a monk-convention of sorts in one of the venues and Ray and his tuk-tuk driver stopped there for a coffee.

"What's your name?" Ray asked the tuk-tuk driver when he returned.

"Sombat."

"Business slow this year?"

"Yes, we had big flood. Your government tells people not to come here."

"Ah yes, we had a travel alert going to Thailand, but I decided to chance it and so far I've had no troubles." Ray felt a sudden pang of compassion for the locals of Ayutthaya, as they were probably heavily dependent on tourism. He resolved to give a big tip later.

Then they were back on the tourist trail, the city was not big in modern terms, though it must have been grand in its peak. The highlight of the day was perhaps the immense reclining Buddha, located slightly away from the city centre; while the most eerie was the head of the Buddha submerged amongst the tentacles of a huge Banyan Tree at Wat Phra Maharat.

Evening came and having parted with Sombat, who was delighted having received a big tip, Ray was alone in this sleepy town. It was a stark contrast to Bangkok. He went to a nearby restaurant which featured a piano and advertised live music for later that evening. It seemed like a good plan to party a bit, in light of the fact that he had already seen the sights. It was still early in the evening and the place was quite empty. Ray could pick and choose any table and he took one next to a window.

"Hey," said a neat looking man in his early twenties as he approached Ray's table and offered a look of recognition.

"Um, pleased to meet you, I'm Ray. I can't place you exactly though, did we meet in Bangkok?"

"Oops, sorry mate. I guess you don't recognize me without the beads and beard. I am Simon."

"Wow! What a contrast!" It was 'The Backpacker'

"This is my mate Neil, the piano player tonight," said Simon introducing his friend.

Neil had an artist look to him with slightly long wavy hair and pointed fingers; wearing a flowery beach shirt. He explained that he was from London and had been on the road for a year. "I've now been resting in Ayutthaya for a month now, I was really travel-weary after a year."

"Really?"

"Yes, after a while I thought that the sights were flashing past me and I decided to stay in one place and find myself. Ayutthaya is not exactly happening, but it's cheap and I get my drinks and food for free here if I play the piano."

"Sounds excellent."

"Well yeah, they can't hire me without a work-permit and that's quite difficult to get, so this barter service for food and drinks works quite well."

"And tonight we drink!" added Simon.

"Cheers to that," said Ray.

The place started getting full while the guys had their food. Ray had ordered a fried cashew nut and chicken stir-fry with jasmine rice. "You have a good barter deal Neal, the food is superb here."

"Yeah, the alcohol is local rum though, but it does the trick."

True to word, after Simon and Ray had settled their bills, the owner came around with a bottle of rum. The rum was pretty potent and together with the after dinner dip; Ray was nodding happily like a silent Trappist Monk.

Neil was an advanced piano player, a decent singer and a great entertainer. He started with a rendition of 'The piano man' from Billy Joel. Thereafter he sang a couple of songs and then joined the boys for a break.

"Bravo," said Ray.

"Thanks mate, though back in London I had someone accompanying on the vocals."

"Well I could accompany you," said Ray feeling brave under the influence of the local Rum.

"That's cool, so you can sing?"

"I played in a musical a couple of years back. Nowadays I am an accomplished shower-cap singer."

"Let's do a duet then. Which song do you want?"

"How about 'Country Roads take me home'?"

"That's prehistoric man."

"As am I. You want me to sing Adele or Pink?" said Ray with a wink. "Afraid that I don't know many lyrics of the songs nowadays."

They picked up a classic oldie, Jamaican Farewell by Harry Belafonte and soon the place was swaying to the beats of this easy melody. The crowd started singing along and the noise in turn attracted other passers-by and soon, the place was jammed.

The rum in turn kept coming during the breaks. Simon joined the show by singing along, and the entertainment started resembling a bad karaoke evening. The boys were quite wasted by the end of the night.

Luckily Ray's accommodation was at crawling distance. Ray bid adieu to his mates and decided to take a quick shower as the evening had been quite humid.

"Holy crap," he shouted out loud as cold water came out of the shower. The countryside did not have warm water and warm though it was outside, it was quite a shock and quite sobering.

The next morning Ray woke up to the sounds of roosters crowing. It felt really rustic where he was staying and he surprisingly had no hangover. It was almost midday so he sauntered into the sleepy town and looked around the shops. Brunch consisted of loads of fresh fruits, cereal and yogurt. Satisfied and with no energy to do much more, Ray went for a Thai massage.

In due time, he reached the station with its makeshift platforms to await the train to Chiang Mai. He got into a conversation with a German bloke who was coming from the islands in the south and spoke of tales of wild full moon parties. Full moon parties, it seemed, had become something of a cult-thing which attracted backpackers like bees to honey.

The train arrived; it was of much better quality than the local train he had taken before. He had the upper berth in his compartment and his fellow travellers were Thai.

"Sawadee khrap," said Ray.

"Sawadee kha," said the smartly dressed Thai woman. "You speak very good Thai."

'The Thais are very charming', thought Ray

She explained that the ordinary Thai man did not pronounce the 'khr' sound; faute de mieux, it either is a 'khlap' or a 'kap'. The 'khr' was therefore somewhat posh Thai, that is, only the higher educated could pronounce it well.

Ray realised that that could explain why random people (vendors, police or monks) would also clap their hands together when Ray would say 'Sawadee khrap' accompanied with the namaste hand-gesture.

Night came and Ray slept like a baby with the rocking motion of the train. It was freezing cold at night, as the air-conditioning was turned on full. He remembered the advice from his friend Karin who had said to always carry a shawl to protect from a sore throat. Luckily he had heeded that advice and wrapped around the shawl and covers around his neck and body.

In the morning, Ray went for breakfast in the pantry compartment. It was old-world charm at its best as he was greeted by the server cum cook, who was fully dressed in a neat uniform. Ray sat down in one of the pantry seats and ordered toast with omelette and jam.

He enjoyed his sumptuous breakfast as the train winded its way through beautiful mountainous territory. The view sometimes was an expansive valley underneath and sometimes the train would be flanked on both sides by high imposing peaks.

They reached Chiang Mai in the late morning and, disembarking from the train, the passengers were accosted by the usual touts. Ray took a hotel room at the SK House; it seemed decent on the photos and it was half the price of the one in Bangkok. Reaching his room, he found it was a proper room with an attached bathroom and the hotel complex even had a swimming pool.

Lonely Planet (LP) had said of this city, "If Chiang Mai were a person, it would be Bob Dylan." LP's take was that Chiang Mai's charm lay on the combination of history and a hippy vibe.

Ray liked the laidback ambience of this northern city. The past week had been very hectic. A friend of Ray's, Peter, lived in Chiang Mai. Peter was originally Australian, born to Dutch parents. The two had been good friends in the time Peter has also been living in Utrecht. Then Peter had gone on a round the world trip for more than a year and had eventually set up base in Chiang Mai, where he taught English. Ray texted Peter and they arranged to meet for that evening. Ray showered, deposited his dirty clothes for laundry washing and went for a small foray of the city.

It was quite a compact city and Ray sauntered aimlessly, entering a Wat or two. He went to the food stalls in the street for a meal amongst the locals. He asked for Chicken with Basil, which was extremely tasty and hot, left him sweating and with a nice burning sensation in his mouth. His fellow local eaters were smiling and nodding at him and he nodded back, waving his hands before his mouth to indicate the hotness. They all laughed heartily.

Evening came and he waited in the hotel lobby for Peter to arrive. Peter eventually arrived on a scooter, which made a very funny picture. Peter had a very tall frame and it looked like he hardly fit on a tiny scooter. He was a blond guy, though now thinning a bit on the hairline and had tanned quite a lot from his life in the tropics. Back in the Utrecht days he was slim, now he bore a slight paunch probably from all the good food, truly integrated into local life. The friends hugged and settled down for a beer.

"So, you've also embarked on a discovery tour?" asked Peter.

"A tad less self discovery than yours. Last I heard, you were in an Indian ashram?"

"Yeah man, I discovered my spiritual self during my travels and spent time meditating in an ashram. So, how's the rat race?"

Peter and Ray had once been colleagues at one of Ray's previous companies.

"It goes well I think, I'm taking a break from it," smiled Ray. "Remember the good old days when we would have appelbol's at Graf Floris?"

"Of course! It was great to live in the centre, we could be at Graf's in fifteen minutes . . . we had a nice expat group then eh?"

"Some of the best years of my life. First you left, then suddenly almost everyone went either travelling or back to their home countries. I was suddenly left friendless in Utrecht."

"The vagaries of an expat group."

"True true. I decided then to make more local friends."

". . . and found a lady-love?" Peter winked at Ray.

"Well, yes and no. I was seriously involved for a couple of years but it didn't work out. Now, in my mid-thirties and still single."

"We all need to go through our route in life," said Peter sanguinely.

Peter took Ray to a haunt of local expats; it was near a restaurant the university and they served Western food. Watching Peter interact with the other expats took Ray back to his initial years in the Netherlands.

"What about you Peter, you found your lady-love?"

Peter had always been a ladies man. He grinned and said, "No man, still the stray I was."

The rest if the evening was spent reminiscing about the old times and catching up. Towards the later part of the evening, the restaurant staff girls joined their table. They knew Peter quite well, by the looks of it.

"This in my mate Ray, from the Netherlands. These are Sunshine and Ann."

"Oh, you look a bit Asian," said Sunshine

"That's because I am originally from India."

"Are you Buddhist?"

"No, am Hindu, but they are quite close."

They arranged to go out a couple of nights from then, which would be the weekend. Peter had to teach during the week of course. Ray suddenly realized that he had lost concept of which day of the week it was. Everyday was a Sunday!

"You should do a cooking course; there are a few schools near your hotel," suggested Peter on the way back.

"Sounds like a great plan. Course by day, chill by evening."

"So, see you in a couple of days. We'll go partying with the locals."

Sleeping in the hotel in Chiang Mai was much quieter than in Bangkok, plus the comfort of not going out to a common bathroom in the middle of the night made for a good night rest. Ray needed a long sleep as he was somewhat of a light sleeper and hadn't really slept well in his first weeks of his journey.

Roosters signalled morning again the next day and Ray woke up well rested. SK House was on one of the small streets (called Soi) off Moon Muang, the main traveller's hub. Chiang Mai had an old city centre which formed a square bounded by a wall and a moat to protect against the ancient Burmese invaders. He went looking for cooking schools and eventually chose a full day course at the BaanThai cooking school for the next day. The course was going to be held in the city centre and involved visiting local markets and then cooking from the freshly bought food.

Ray spent the day doing nothing in particular and doing it rather well. 'I'm getting the hang of travelling for long stretches,' he thought with a smile.

He went to the internet café around the corner from the hotel and started planning for further on his journey. First stop was to the south of Thailand and thereafter to Cambodia via road and thereafter to Vietnam. Checking his papers though, he had a nasty jolt . . . the visa for Vietnam. He had ordered a sort of pre-visa via the internet and it was valid for a month. On the application he had chosen the date of sixth January and he assumed that he could travel to Vietnam and the visa validity would for a month from the date of first entry, as is normally the case for visa on arrival. However he examined and re-examined the instructions and it seemed that the visa would only be valid till fifth February irrespective on the date of entry.

The woman who ran the internet café also doubled as a travel operator as frequently happened in these parts and was a very hearty lady. Seeing the disconcert on Ray's face, she started talking to him and offered him advice. "You go to Vietnam first and then to Cambodia," she said sagely.

That meant that he would have to fly to Vietnam over Cambodia. Air Asia had a cheap option, so he decided on this course of action. He also decided on a flight from Chiang Mai to Phuket to avoid spending two days in transit with the bus or train and an overnight stay in Bangkok. He bought the tickets, which gave him some sense of comfort as he now knew his general route.

Having settled his travels for the near future, he went to the local eating joint on the street corner. There he ran into a friendly American couple he had talked to briefly in Bangkok while staying at the Shanti Lodge. They had travelled to Vietnam before Thailand and gave him the heads up on the route they had done and the places that were worth checking out.

Morning came and Ray felt rested again, he was at home with this relaxed gem of a town where Monks drove scooters and people moved in a leisurely pace.

He had a fresh fruit breakfast at a market on the way to the BaanThai School and arrived there just on time. The other participants also rolled in shortly thereafter.

"Sawadee kha," greeted the owner of the school. Their chef teacher would be Tom, a thick-set young guy who obviously enjoyed his food. Tom was his English name; he said his original name was unpronounceable.

The fellow classmates introduced themselves. There was an older couple from Singapore and there were two Catherine's in the class, one from Malaysia and another from Norway.

"Kathrine with a 'K'," said the Norwegian one. She was quite an attractive and petite brunette, with a tanned look and exquisite features and high cheek bones, which gave her a bit of a regal look, which contrasted with her laidback clothes.

"I wouldn't guess that you were from Norway," ventured Ray.

"Why? Because I am not blond? Quite a few of us aren't!"

"Ah, no, not quite. You look somewhat southern European."

They were all given the choice of things to make. Ray chose to make Spring rolls, Fried Fish cake, Deep fried banana, Chiang Mai Noodles on the basis of red curry paste and Stir fried Cashew nut with Chicken. The group went to the market to buy the ingredients.

Tom explained the herbs and vegetables with a passion that correlated to the size of his smiling Buddha belly. They bought from quite a few vendors who smiled benevolently while Tom held his speeches. Finally the bags were loaded with Thai basil, various types of mushrooms, garlic, ginger, a variety of chillies, limes and kaffir lime leaves, eggplant and lemongrass. The whole spices (cardamom, cloves, star anise, cumin, coriander and nutmeg), meat and the fish had already been bought, Tom explained.

Back at the BaanThai School, the men were put to the grind literally, to make the curry pastes. Ray got the task to make the red curry paste, while the ladies got the task of preparing the batter for the fish cakes and fried bananas.

Then they all learnt to roll a spring roll.

"We use sunflower oil for deep-frying," said Tom. He added, "You should cook the bananas first, then the spring roll and thereafter fish-cake, otherwise it will all smell of fish."

"What happens if we forget the correct order?"

"Then put lemongrass in the hot oil that will help cleanse the smell."

Ray was the only one who had opted for Chicken with Cashew nuts. It was quite easy to make; first heating the oil, browning the cashew nuts and then taking these out separately.

Tom explained further, "Next fry the garlic a bit, add the sliced chicken pieces until cooked. Add a bit of water, Jelly mushroom, sliced onions, baby corn and dried chilli and stir on high flame."

After that had been done, he continued, "Add a bit of oyster sauce, pungent fish sauce and a bit of sugar. Add some spring onions and the already cooked cashew nuts."

Voilà, it was ready to eat.

All the food was put on the low lying table and they all sat on a mat on the ground to eat. Everything was very delicious with the fresh ingredients. Thai food was relatively easier to make than Indian, the latter involves a larger variety of spices added in a particular order. The main difference was perhaps in the use of readymade sauces (oyster, soya, mushroom and fish) and pastes (shrimp and roasted chilli) in the Thai cuisine.

"Have you been travelling long?" asked Kathrine of Ray after they had finished the first part of the delicious meal.

"For a couple of weeks now. You?"

"Couple of months. I was in Indonesia, then Malaysia, now in Thailand since a month ago or so."

"What are you doing afterwards?"

"I was thinking of doing a meditation course at one of the Wat's. Do you want to join me?"

"Umm," Ray was torn between the charm of joining this lovely girl, but sitting silently in meditation. "Know what, I'll walk you to the Wat."

The meal was delicious and took a few hours to taste everything. Towards the end Ray was feeling like he would have to unbutton his jeans in order to accommodate his expanded belly but luckily the meal came to an end.

"Perhaps we could explore the city together tomorrow?" said Ray as he dropped off Kathrine at a Wat.

"Sure."

They met in the morning and explored the city the whole day. Ray bought his first souvenirs, silk sleeping gear, which would be lighter to carry than his Bermuda shorts. He also bought some lavender massage cream. The camera absolutely loved Kathrine and Ray took quite a few photos of her while she played tourist.

The temples were much quieter and less touristy than those of Bangkok or Ayutthaya. Among others, they visited the Wat where the Emerald Buddha had originally seated. In one of the temples, a monk was giving a lecture and devotees were washing the feet of another monk. Ray bowed from a distance with his hands in the Namaste form and Kathrine imitated his action.

"So this is what you did yesterday?" asked Ray.

"No, it was in a quiet room in another temple, people were meditating in the dark. Quite intense actually, do you meditate regularly?"

"Why, because I am Indian?" Ray winked. "Have never done any meditating actually."

It was quite a warm, sunny and humid day outside. "Ah, I look forward to the swimming pool at the guest house," said Ray

"Wow, you have a pool? Can I come there?"

"Sure." His sweet spot for Daphne was beginning to diminish somewhat.

They parted ways and Ray showered and put on his best swimming trunks and awaited Kathrine at the pool. The temperature was perfect, cooler than the day outside, yet not too cold.

She arrived, a sarong draped over her bikini. "Oh so nice," she said as she joined him in the pool.

"Sure is, I'm looking forward to the Thai Islands when I fly down to Phuket tomorrow."

"They are very nice. I am a bit anxious; I'm going to meet my boyfriend from Australia tomorrow."

Ray heard glass breaking, but realized it was a sound in his head.

"Um boyfriend?"

"Long distance relationship, don't ask! We met in Australia last year when I was studying and travelling there. We've had this on-off thing since and now we're meeting here. Perhaps I'll go on to Oz or he'll come to Norway."

With that cleared up, they spent the evening chit-chatting, had dinner and Ray wished her the best of luck. He dressed up for going out and soon he was in a Tuk-tuk with Peter to hit the nightlife in Chiang Mai. The place they went to was open air with a dance space in a corner and tables spread around in no particular order. The majority of the populace was local with the exception of Peter and his expat friends. The colourful drinks were being served in long glass tubes with a small tap in the end, which resembled the ones used for inhaling exotic gases. Peter's party ordered one of the cocktail samples. Thereafter the local girls from the restaurant joined them and soon the sound of the adjoining music was drowned by the loud laughter of silly jokes. That changed however, when the music started playing a Merengue classic "Suavemente." Both Peter and Ray had taken Salsa and Merengue dancing lessons back in the days and they were happily dancing with Sunshine and Ann respectively. Middle of the song they changed partners, to which the girls giggled endlessly.

"Just like the good old days at Winkel van Sinkel eh?" shouted Peter above the din.

Hours passed by chatting, laughing and drinking exotic coloured fluids.

"This is a good life you have mate," said Ray

"Yeah man, though sometimes I yearn to get back into the professional life," said Peter sanguinely.

"Well some guy told me the other day that we all have to follow our routes in life," said Ray with a wink referring to the advice Peter had given him the other day.

Between then and the next morning at the airport was a bit of a blur in Ray's memory; however he made it to the airport on time and took a double espresso to wake up. The coffee beans in this region were superb and they perked him up till he took the flight.

He reflected that though Peter's life was nice and laid-back, it would not suit him in the long-run. It was a mental cross-off from his list of discoveries about travelling and himself.

He settled in his seat and was out like a light.

The islands of Thailand

Ray landed in Phuket in the late morning. He was quite groggy from the partying of the night before. He had read the Lonely Planet on the flight and decided on a hotel called Kata-on-sea. Though it was described as being hardly on the sea and a steep climb to reach it; it boasted of spacious bungalows at a decent price.

The airport to the city bus started meandering its way to the centre. Phuket did not feel like an island at all; there was no sign of a coast to be seen. It had a lush tropical tree-line and was the largest island in Thailand.

On the way to the centre, the bus stopped at the 'official' tourist centre. Everyone on the bus had to get off and show their tickets to an 'official'. The travellers were herded in pairs and Ray found himself sitting next to a rather attractive redhead. The 'official', a smart looking Thai woman examined their tickets, gave a broad smile and then rattled off with a cross-sales pitch about the tours of the nearby islands.

"The tickets are very limited and I can offer you a special price now, only two thousand baht per person," she explained helpfully.

'Charming method, spring 'em when they are tired,' thought Ray who had by now lots of experience in the diverse scamming and coaxing methods. He started nodding his head in a 'no' manner when the redhead inquired, "Sounds quite nice, are you going too? I just landed in Phuket from cold Europe and have a three week holiday, so want to see as much as possible."

'It's a scam,' Ray wanted to say, however that instinct was subdued by his desire to spend a day with the lovely girl. So, he proceeded with the next best course of action, which was negotiating.

"The tour does sound nice, but expensive for my backpacker's budget," he said to her with a slanted eye towards the 'official'.

"I give you good discount," the 'official' said helpfully.

"My Lonely Planet says that these tours are for thousand baht with a pick-up service and should be best booked from Phuket town."

"Oh, this is special price for Christmas," the 'official' persevered with a smile.

"Christmas is three days away, so if we go tomorrow or day after, what special price will you offer for two people?" Ray said flashing his dimples.

In the end they settled for twelve hundred baht per person including pick-up and lunch. The 'official' disappeared into the back office to get their tickets.

The redhead was sufficiently impressed and said with a glee, "Wow, I can never do that!"

"You learn quickly around here. I'm Ray," he said stretching his hand.

"Hilary. Nice to meet you."

"Nice to meet you too. Irish, I am guessing?"

"Was it my red hair or my accent that gave me away?"

"A bit of both."

"Where you want the bus pick you up?" said the 'official'; returning to the desk with two tickets.

"Umm, I plan to stay at Kata-on-sea," said Ray.

"You have a booking?" asked Hilary.

"Nah, not yet. I'll just look and if I don't like it, there are other guest-houses in the neighbourhood."

"You can pick me up too at Kata-on-sea," said Hilary to the official decidedly.

"I hope that you like it, it's on the Lonely Planet South-East Asia on a Shoestring, so probably not very fancy," Ray said while walking back together to the bus.

"Oh don't worry, I am travelling cheap too, it's my first vacation since I started working earlier this year."

After a drive through Phuket town they were dropped off the main road along Kata beach next to a road sign indicating "Kata-on-sea" and pointing heavenwards.

"Pff, that's steep," Ray said while mounting with his backpack. He realized that he was far from being in perfect condition, huffing and puffing and sweating like an otter in more than thirty degrees Celsius heat.

"Travelling quite light for a girl," he said while stopping to catch his breath.

"I've packed just very itsy-bitsy bikinis," she grinned mischievously.

The climb was worth it. They stood at the entrance hall overlooking the old-style bungalows and a swimming pool. The proprietor came out and the usual bargaining proceeded. Ray got it down to five hundred baht per night per bungalow and wanted to inspect the accommodation.

"A bit too early to share eh?" she whispered.

Ray was aware that he was blushing and replied with an affirmative nod.

The bungalows were spacious and clean, as indicated by LP and decided to take them for two nights.

"I'm gonna change and head for the sea wherever it is," said Ray.

"I'll join you."

The Kata beach was a ten minutes and on the way they observed numerous restaurants, souvenir shops and massage parlours. Gone were the days when there used to be huts and simple accommodation right on the beach. Phuket had been discovered by the Russians, who came in great droves during this time of the year.

'It was probably the same distance to West Europe, though it was much cheaper and warmer weather here,' thought Ray.

They arrived on the beach and stopped in their tracks, dazed by the brilliance; emerald green clear water and a fine white sandy beach stretching for miles. Ray could understand why this was one of the most popular beaches in the world!

It was relatively sparsely populated compared to the beaches of Europe in full season. Further away on the water were small colourful fishing boats and other slightly bigger ones with what seemed like diving groups.

"Very tasteful," said Ray whilst setting up his sarong on the beach.

"Very!" said Hilary while revealing an itsy-bitsy bikini after setting up and disposing her oversized T-shirt.

"If you want, you can go take a dip first while I watch over the stuff," he said as he settled down and picked up a P.G. Wodehouse book. A quarter of an hour later, he was distracted by the sight of Hilary coming towards him. Her very white skin was glistening and her hips swayed as she tiptoed quickly across the hot sand.

'Young girl, get out of my mind,' were the chords of the song which filled Ray's brain.

"Oh, so lovely the warm water and the sun; I'll be getting freckles soon!"

"I'll be getting browner."

"So jealous, I hardly tan, at best turn deep-red sometimes."

"You should then put some sun lotion."

"Will you put some on my back?"

Ray was conscious of his blood pumping vigorously as he massaged her back; so proceeded quickly to the water to cool off. A short swim later, he stretched himself on the sarong with his back to the sun and gave way to his tiredness.

He woke up after an hour or so as the sun was setting down.

"You really snore, glad we're not sharing a room!" said Hilary laughing.

"Ha, I snore when I've had too much to drink or too little sleep and in this case it's both!"

It was getting darker and they made their way back to the hotel.

"Quick shower, then go for dinner?" said Ray

"Sounds like a plan!"

Standing under the shower, Ray realized another reason why the bungalows were this cheap, there was only cold water on offer!

Refreshed, he went to the entrance. He looked onto some teenagers splashing at the pool.

"Wonder why they don't go to the sea," said Hilary as she joined him. She was looking rather lovely in a white button-down shirt and a pink top underneath.

They went to a fish restaurant where they could choose their own live fish. They both chose Pomfret on Ray's suggestion, this white fish was one of his favourites while growing up in India. Hilary opted for a sweet and sour sauce while Ray went for the spicy one. It was absolutely delicious and they had a fabulous dinner. A thing struck him just like the beauty of the beach; the place was teeming with Russians.

He remarked that to Hilary who said she'd heard about that from her friends.

"I guess it's as far as the West European beaches for the Russians and probably more economical."

"Wonder if it'll resemble the Ibiza of the East in a decade?"

After dinner, she wanted to go to the 'Aussie bar'. "It's recommended by friends of mine, c'mon let's go there."

"Ok, but just for one drink, I am pretty wasted from yesterday."

They met with some other backpackers there and started chatting. He downed his drink and went to leave, "I'll see you in the morning."

"Breakfast at eight?"

"Perfect," Ray said longing to stay longer with Hilary. He was quite happy that she wanted to spend more time with him but was absolutely wasted at that moment.

Ray made his way back to the bungalow, an activity which had taken an increasing complex nature in the dark. Ray managed avoiding hitting his toes, which were jutting out of his flip-flops, on the rocks and diverse flora and fauna on the way. Soon after, the bungalow was reverberating from his snoring.

✦

Ray woke up with a start, it was almost eight in the morning. He quickly put on a T-shirt above his newly bought silk sleeping Bermuda pants and pandered to the central area lobby-cum-breakfast place. Hilary was already there, looking quite bright, hardly as someone who had partied the night before.

"That's quite risqué," she said laughing and pointing to his silk pants.

"Oops."

"You look like you just got out of bed!"

"I just did. Gonna quickly eat breakfast and do the three S's."

"Three S's?"

"Shit, shower and shave," Ray said with a smirk.

"Ugh, more info than I needed."

He did so and thereafter they made their way down to the main road hoping that the bus would be there. It was there, true to form, and the small rickety bus took the passengers to the port where they were re-distributed to speedboats. They made their way quickly to the front of the speedboat to get the best seats. They were joined by a Norwegian family and a Swiss and Italian couple.

"Whale family," whispered Hilary while giggling, referring to their size.

"In Hindi, we say 'khata-pitta khandan,' which mean a well fed family," he laughed back.

The family and the couples were very jovial though. Soon the boat was cutting through the waves, it made for a exhilarating ride reverberating like the beats of the recently seen Harry Potter movie song, "It's gonna be a bumpy ride."

"Oh, my back hurts, I think I got burnt sleeping in the sun yesterday," said Ray as he felt the Sun's rays.

"Serves you right for not putting suntan lotion."

They went to Ko Phi-Phi Leh, which was where the film "The beach" was shot. The Island was uninhabited, due to a more profitable business of harvesting swiftlets nests for medicinal purposes. It was truly breathtaking, with limestone cliffs rising out of the emerald-green water and a stretch of fine white grain beach made famous by the film.

"In the footsteps of Leo!" said Hilary

"It's funny to see the ways the different nationalities pose eh?" said Ray

"How's that?"

"The Japanese girls for instance do the V for victory sign; I'm quite used to that. Now I am seeing the Russian and Indian way of posing. The Russian girls are for instance looking sideways and coyly into the camera while stretching out the palm of their hand in front of the object they are posing with."

". . . and the Indian men are posing in the stand-at-ease military position with their arms behind their back and their chins held up," laughed Daphne

The next stop was Phi-phi Don, the main Island, also a sensational skyline of curves in the tropical waters. They stopped for lunch there.

"Wow, this is so gorgeous, I would love to come back here! Wanna come back?" suggested Hilary.

"Great idea! In a couple of days, perhaps great for spending Christmas here or do you want to be in Phuket with a fancy dinner?"

"I think I'd rather be here."

"So, perhaps do some more island discovery tomorrow and come back here on Xmas eve?"

They booked two huts at a hotel, which was quite close to the water. They all went back to the boat which rolled up a bit further down the coast and most of them went snorkelling whilst Ray, who had never learnt to swim, enjoyed the Sun and took photos. Then they went to a small island which was devoid of trees and other formation and only consisted of a beach and beach bars.

"This is the good life," said Ray decidedly and Hilary nodded in appreciation.

It had been a great day, so they decided to go on another tour the next day, this time to visit the other side of Phuket and also the famous James Bond Island.

Back in Phuket, after showering and dressing for the evening in lighter clothes, they contemplated their dinner choices.

Ray, who wanted some change from the Thai cuisine, suggested an all-you-could eat BBQ.

"Macho!" said Hilary.

Ray tried to imitate a macho look to which Hilary started laughing. "Your face is like a book of patterns, has anyone told you that?"

"I've been told that I have an expressive face."

The dinner was very sumptuous, with fish, chicken, beef and pork marinated in fresh Thai sauces being on the palate.

"I feel like a tiger now," said Ray polishing off the last of his plate.

"I am so stuffed; don't think I can move much anymore."

"So no party tonight?"

"I want to get a facial. Wanna join?"

"Why not?"

They went to a beauty parlour.

"Kawadee Kha; facial for lady?" asked the cheerful beautician.

"Also for the man?" Ray said with a smile.

The beautician giggled and seated both in adjoining chairs. Soon they were under a mask and steam.

"Oh wow, this is really good," said Ray after the mask was taken off and the face was massaged. "Much more relaxing than a hard Thai massage."

"You should do it more often."

An hour later and feeling absolutely lazy, from the active day and the facial, the pair hit the sack in their respective bungalows.

They were up early the next day again for the trip. This time, they had a long bus trip of a couple of hours where they were entertained with the James Bond film, "The Man with the Golden Gun" in which this previously undiscovered Island had appeared.

The first stop of the tour was a cave with a large reclining Buddha. The caves were the haunt of monkeys, at the sight of which Hilary clung to Ray. Thereafter the tour continued to the waterfront where they were transferred to a small boat. There was a small boat fitted with a motor; a stark contrast to the speed boat of the previous day.

The first stop was a small Muslim floating village, the guide explained. It was not exactly floating, rather on stilts and the main livelihood was fishing and tourism. They had lunch there and continued to James Bond Island. The area around the Island had since been converted into a marine national park. It had been littered with waste due to increased tourism following the film and the Thai government was trying to insert controls.

The day passed pleasantly, the pair had food and drinks and chatted about favourite colours, hobbies and pastimes. They went out to party at the Oz bar in the night.

"Let's sleep in tomorrow?" suggested Hilary

"Yeah, good plan, see you for brunch."

Next day in the late afternoon they took a boat to go back and stay at Ko phi-phi Don for a couple of days.

✦

Phi-phi Don looked even nicer in the dusk when they reached it, with a crimson sky looming against the cliff and casting all hues on the emerald green water.

"Well, if it isn't Ray!" shouted a voice full of camaraderie.

Ray recognised him immediately as the American dude he'd first met at the Shanti Lodge in Bangkok, but his mind was blank to his name.

"Hey man! How've you been since Bangkok?" said Ray.

"Excellent man; came down straight here with the night bus and ferry and have been making merry since. Hullo, who's the pretty lady? I am Tom."

"Hilary, pleased to meet you."

"This is my local friend, Amoy," said Tom pointing to a cheerful looking fella with long hair and a guitar hung across his neck.

"Happy hour, wait till you see the buckets here man, will knock you out"

Ray looked inquiringly, Hilary explained, "A bucket of local drinks mixed with local juice, very popular on the islands."

This was the Thailand Islands Ray had always imagined, a small hut near the water, camp-fire and song and dance. After dropping their stuff at their respective huts, Hilary and Ray joined the others for a barbeque and later they made a small fire and started singing to the accompaniment of Amoy's guitar.

"Did you meet with the Belgians again Tom?" asked Ray.

"Nah, I stayed on a coupe of days at Shanti and then came down here directly. I believe they are on the East coast; they wanted to go for the full moon parties. Are you going?"

"Nope. Everything's pretty much booked and I heard there are big waves on the beaches on Ko Phangan. Plus I like it on this coast."

"I can see why," said Tom winking and looking at Hilary.

"I am very sleepy, after two nights of partying and still with a severe jet-lag, I think I am going to my hut," said Hilary looking at Ray with a smile.

"Fine, I am going to drink a few more buckets here," slurred Ray. He was happy to see Tom, the first of his backpacking buddies.

A few hours, buckets and loud songs later, the party broke up gradually. Ray stumbled his way back towards the huts, about two hundred meters away. Halfway through, he tripped over a rock and fell into the water.

"We will, we will rock you," he sang appropriately and deliriously. He was not hurt as he had fallen in the soft sand though his drunken pride was a bit wounded. He reached his hut, #14, he had managed to remember well, he considered.

Only moments later, he was confronted with the strange discomfort which comes to an inebriated man when feeling his pockets for the keys and finding none.

"Oh shit, must have fallen in the water, merde, merde, merde." He wondered why he was swearing in French though; alcohol must have confused his mind.

As he stood there swaying under the effects of the buckets and trying to piece together a course of action, he was aware that one of the cabins was lit. The tide was rising with the moon and as he felt it around his ankles, he considered the beach no place to sleep. So, he made his way towards the lit hut, trying to think of what to say.

He knocked and whispered hoarsely, "Anyone there?" The singing had taken its toll on his voice.

The door opened to reveal Hilary in nothing but a white T-Shirt. "I thought you'd never come!" she said rushing to him and covering him in kisses.

The night passed and the next morning Ray awoke with the Sun in his face and a pounding in his head.

"Merry Christmas."

The pounding increased rapidly. He was conscious that his clothes were conspicuous by their absence.

"Did we . . . ?" he trailed

"What you don't remember, it was such a wonderful way to begin Christmas!"

"Of course, of course, I meant . . . did we leave the window open?"

"Oh poor you, are you cold?" she said while snuggling up and started humming, "All I want for Christmas is you."

Ray considered what to do . . . while she was young she seemed keen on a vacation romance. He decided to go along with the flow and was transformed into a free-wheeling backpacker in the next couple of days in the presence of this lovely girl. It was a vacation romance supreme, as they wandered the beaches hand in hand with their toes in the sand occasionally singing cheesy romantic songs. This was a nice side to backpacking.

"So what next?" he said one fine afternoon.

"Shall we head to Bangkok and do some cultural stuff?"

"Umm sure, I meant what next for us?"

"I guess you'll continue with your backpacking and I'll head back home."

"Umm yes I guess."

'We'll keep in touch and if you come to Ireland, give me a shout."

Back to Bangkok it was.

The return of the Monk

Hilary and Ray took the night bus to Bangkok; it was his first time on a night bus in Thailand. As his friends had warned him that the air-conditioning would be turned on full, Ray took along his saffron-coloured shawl he had bought in India. Luckily the bus company also provided a blanket.

The bus left at about half-past six. His stomach was growling with hunger, he devoured a pack of chips he'd bought just for snacks. The travel agent had told them that the ticket included dinner, so after waiting patiently till about ten, Ray put in his earplugs and sleeping mask and dozed off to sleep. Hilary kept twisting and turning next to him, but eventually seemed to find some rest stretching on Ray's shoulders. It was a bit cold to fall into deep slumber and on top of that Ray was already dreading when he would have to part with Hilary. He had the tendency to be become intense and close in a short period of time.

"Wake up," said Hilary shaking him gently and awakening him from his slumber.

"Wha . . . ?"

"We've stopped for dinner."

Ray looked at his watch and said, "It's midnight! Crazy operators."

The place they'd stopped was in the middle of nowhere it seemed but specially catering to the inter-city buses, but it was a bustling joint of restaurants, shops and rest-rooms. The occupants of every bus were led in groups to tables and served soup and rice with an accompanying dish. Their bus-group consisted of locals who savoured the served dish whilst the foreigners from the group apprehensively took a bite from the pungent smelling dish. Ray was hungry so he gobbled it down without smelling it. It was actually quite tasty, some sort of fish dish cooked probably in pungent fish-sauces. Thereafter they headed back to the bus, Hilary and Ray dozed off again in each others arms and when they woke up again, they had reached Bangkok in the early morning.

"You want tuk-tuk," was the familiar chant when they departed the bus. Ray smiled and after the usual haggling, they went on to the Shanti Lodge. The reception was not yet open, so they dropped off their bags in storage and went to a roadside stall for breakfast. This was the time of the day when the monks would go about collecting food. This was a first for Ray as he had previously not woken up early enough to experience it. There was a bit of a nip in the air, especially after the warm South Thailand Islands and Ray gladly wrapped his shawl around. The vendors seemed somewhat hesitant when he asked how much the food cost, which he thought was a bit strange. In the end they sat down in a busy stall and were served.

Little schoolchildren were being paraded by their mothers off to school. People offering food to the monks bowed and prayed, to which the Monks benevolently raised their hand in the 'Da' form. The Da is the form with the palm of the right hand facing outwards and upwards.

Then the 'venerable Monk' appeared. He was an old Monk, sizeable in proportion and everyone seemed to want to give him food and ask for his blessings. Ray, from his sitting position made a slight bow and then the strangest of things happened, the Monk bowed back.

"What just happened?" he said in bewilderment.

"Have you looked at yourself? You look like a photocopy of a monk," said Hilary laughing out loud.

As a child Ray had been a great fan of Martial arts movies, one of his favourite being 'The 36th chamber of Shaolin' which traces the story of a young monk who goes to the Shaolin temple to learn martial arts. After learning the skills, the hero goes back to his village to exact revenge and after doing so he returns to the temple and create a new chamber (the Thirty sixth) in the Shaolin temple.

Ray thought of that film and nicknamed this period as "The return of the Monk" to Bangkok in this case. He felt at home returning to the first place of his sabbatical, this time around he took it easy. The staff at Shanti was as friendly as ever and with Hilary by his side he had a lovely time going to the markets, the temples, the palace grounds and being at leisure in general. At the same time though, he was already feeling a bit lonesome at the thought of leaving Hilary. He looked at her and she seemed to display none of that sentiment. He resigned himself to the inevitability of people coming and going in his life.

Then New Year's Eve came. Shanti Lodge was throwing a lavish dinner party so the couple spent the evening there, and thereafter they went to the bridge on the river to watch the fireworks from afar.

"Isn't it lovely?" whispered Ray into Hilary's ear above the dim of the fireworks.

"Very, but I am also a bit scared."

"Well, I'll protect you then," said Ray while putting his arms around her.

"You're a great guy, I will miss you."

"I am already missing you," which sounded a bit like a cliché, but Ray really meant it.

She had however to get back to work and her holidays were coming to an end. On the second of January he escorted her to the airport. After checking in the bags, it was time to part.

"We both knew that this was a temporary situation," she said with tears rolling down her cheeks.

"Yes we did," said Ray choking back his tears.

"I'll follow your blog with attention."

"Send me some photos you took."

"You should come to Ireland."

"And you to the Netherlands."

"We'll keep in touch ok?"

They both knew that these were words to ease the pain and in reality were probably not going to happen, but they said it anyway.

After lingering for a while at the airport trying to collect his thought, Ray went to the sixty fourth floor of the Holiday Inn for a panoramic view of the city. The view was fabulous, the cool wind at that altitude somehow soothed Ray's troubled heart. He took a coffee there and reflected on his relations, from his first crush in school to present-day Hilary. He wondered whether he would ever meet his partner for life. This was the first time he was travelling alone for so long. It was a great journey and being alone had given him the freedom to go where he wanted, when he felt like and do what he desired, besides meeting amazing people and having brilliant experiences. On the other hand the past few days travelling together with a romantic partner had been delightful too. Given the choice, he would probably take the latter option. However, since that option did not exist for a longer period of time he had taken the next best option i.e. travelling alone instead of probably the worst option, which was not to travel at all. This realization gave him a bit of relief.

He then went on a shopping spree at Siam Square, hoping that retail therapy would ease the pain of Hilary's absence. He entered a shopping complex and bought a key-chain cum wallet made of sting-ray leather. Then he went to see a film in the IMAX theatre on the top floor of the complex. While travelling and eating alone had become totally pleasant activities for him, he had the reflection that watching a film alone at the theatre was not his preferred activity. As he left the complex, he looked around looking a bit lost as to what to do next.

A local lady got talking to him asking him where he came from and thereafter the usual questions he had got accustomed to. She worked at the university and Ray asked her about the lifestyle for the locals.

"It's very tough in Bangkok," she said.

"How come?"

"We have long working hours and low pay."

"The people seem to be quite happy though."

"They are not happy where you come from?"

"Hmm, not entirely. I think that's why people from the West are quite often distraught when they come here. They are much richer but the people here are much happier."

"I never considered that. Why are the people there not so happy?"

"The weather is bad, it's quite individualistic and people are all in a hurry, perhaps they are unhappy also because they are afraid to lose their wealth."

She smiled amicably and said, "Here people want to go to the West and there you want to come here."

"To travel and to shop," Ray said with a wink.

"Are you looking to buy something now?"

"I was thinking to getting a tailor-made suit to take back home."

"You won't find that here in Siam Square. I know a good place and can tell a tuk-tuk to take you there."

"That would be great."

She instructed a nearby tuk-tuk and as Ray thanked her, she said, "You are very handsome."

"So are you, thanks once again."

He smiled and reflected that his looks were probably somewhere in-between the locals and the westerners and that made it unique. It was good for his ego and he was slowly feeling better, but he was still missing Hilary dearly.

The cloth shop was run by a few guys of Nepalese origin and his Hindi went down well with the salesman who offered him end of year discounts. There he bought three suit-lengths and five shirt pieces. The tailors were however off work around New Year. Ray had read about the wonderful tailors of Hoi An in Vietnam in the Lonely Planet, so he decided that he would get those made there. He bought a small bag to carry his stuff; since his backpack was already fully loaded.

He also planned to go to Kanchanaburi the next morning to stay a couple of days. The next day however, he was hit with a bad case of the 'Delhi-Belly', which was a bad form of stomach ailment. The girls working at the Shanti Lodge gave him some Chinese pills which they said they also took.

"Why you travel alone?" one of them asked.

"If nobody hears your call, then you have to walk it alone," said Ray, quoting the famous Bengali poet Tagore.

He was feeling miserable and got thinking about the rigours of travelling alone. It obviously had its advantages; more flexibility and the ability to change ones plans and do whatever he liked and not needing to spend all the time with one person. So far he had also been lucky to meet people easily but it also had it numerous disadvantages; at times like this when he was feeling sick or while seeing a breathtaking sight alone. It could be lonely.

'I guess carrying around a Lonely Planet for company is quite apt,' he muttered to himself as he dozed off to sleep, quite weak from his stomach.

He next day he felt on the road to recovery, so decided to go to Kanchanacaburi. He went to the internet store, the proprietor of which was a well rounded woman, a female personification of the laughing Buddha statues he had seen. She also doubled as a travel agent, as was quite common in these parts.

"Ah, Kanchanaburi, bridge on river Kwai . . . you go to Tiger temple too?" she queried.

"What's that? They worship tigers there?" said Ray thinking of rat-temples in India

She laughed jovially; in the process seemed to be shaking the floor and resembling the laughing Buddha statues. "It's where you can see tigers from near who born in temple."

"Sounds cool." He booked a day tour, as he did not have any more time before his flight to Vietnam.

There was an email from Hilary which he read emotionally. She wrote that she was missing him; she had made an electronic card from Ray's photo clad as a saffron-robed monk.

The return of the monk

He wrote back about how much he was missing her too and then retired for the night, resolving to stay far away from girls for the foreseeable future. It was a self-defence mechanism to protect from more heart-break.

It was a two hour ride to Kanchanaburi from Bangkok; the small bus contained an Irish couple, a drunken Aussie, still hung-over from the previous night, two English girls and a large German group besides Ray.

Kanchanaburi became more internationally famous from the movie "Bridge Over the river Kwai." The Japanese imperialists had wanted to connect Burma (Myanmar) by rail to Siam (Thailand) to further continue their conquests in Burma and India. In the most inhumane conditions, POW's and civilians were forced to complete the bridge. Hundreds of thousands died as a result and the allies later bombed and destroyed the bridge.

The first stop was at the cemetery where people paid homage to the fallen soldiers. Next they were taken to the Jeath museum, which was quite a sombre experience. In Europe there is a lot of information about the inhumanities committed by the Nazis that Ray had seen, however this third axis of evil seemed perhaps even crueller.

The solemn experience over, they went to Erawan falls to relax and replace the negative atmosphere. The next stop was the Tiger temple and there was a huge queue once the group had got in. There was an all-American volunteer complete with cowboy hat who was touting those in the queue, asking if they wanted the advanced express lane experience in smaller groups. This was on top of the already hefty entry-fee, so Ray's party decided to just wait a bit longer.

"How commercial eh, no wonder the guides have a mixed opinion about this place," remarked the Aussi bloke.

"Yeah, we heard that they drug the tigers," piped in the English duo.

Ray got talking to a passing Monk, who seemed to be attached to the temple, and asked, "So how does it work?"

"It started when one injured tiger was left behind here and the head Monk took care of him. Then the injured animal's numbers started increasing. Quite a few of the tigers are born here and have never tasted blood or raw meat, only being fed boiled chicken," the monk said in impeccable English.

"And why do they look so um relaxed?" said Ray pointing to one in the distance.

"That is in the afternoon when it is sleeping time. You should see them in the evening, that's when they wake up as it's their natural hunting time."

"In the end, everybody needs to decide for themselves what they believe in," thought Ray and he believed this story as it was better than the other versions. Soon his turn came to go to the tigers. They had to give their camera to the staff that led them around the tigers and took the photos without flash. Ray approached the first tiger in trepidation, and while they had a foot chained for precaution and were semi-dozing, they were still enormous animals. He touched the tiger briefly that made no notice of his feeble attempt. With the next tiger, he was stroking a bit bolder but the third one decided to change sleeping sides. Ray was petrified as the tiger rolled over. The staff guy who was taking the photos for Ray laughed heartily!

They continued the round of tiger patting; by the end Ray was feeling much bolder, stroking them as if they were big-cats.

Tiger temple

It was a surreal experience, though they were dozing, they were still majestic. The group moved on and the last part of the tour was taking the train and passing over the recreated fateful bridge over the river Kwai. It was a rambling train they were on, but the journey was quite picturesque as it made its way through the mountainous countryside.

The Bridge on the River Kwai

The town seemed quite relaxed and Ray wished he had more time than just a day trip, but he was leaving for Vietnam the next day. It felt a bit strange, Thailand was his first destination and he had gotten accustomed to the mild-mannered Thais. Usually, he would be going back home after such a vacation, but this time he was going onwards for new experiences. It made him feel like a true backpacker, without a fixed place to go to, again a mixed feeling experience, on the one hand feeling a bit restless, on the other hand looking forward to the new adventure.

Arriving back in Bangkok, it was peak-traffic hour and the roads were jammed for miles. A man with a bike rolled up along and asked, "Taxi?"

Ray looked around to see if there was a taxi then suddenly realized that the man meant his motorcycle. Traffic seemed to be crawling, so Ray thought 'why not' and hopped on. It was his first time on a motorcycle-taxi and decidedly his last . . . as the driver made his way around traffic, slingering around like a snake, sometime driving quickly into incoming traffic before going back to the correct lane just in-time. Ray closed his eyes at times and he was overjoyed when they reached Shanti Lodge.

He refreshed and headed towards Khaosan Road to relive the gaudy experience one more time. On the way towards it, he thought it would be a good idea also to get a Thai massage once more. His masseuse was a middle-aged woman who did not speak a lot of English. She was quite enthusiastic in her massage however and stretched and cracked Ray's back, as was want of the Thai masseuses. After the massage, Ray went downstairs to pay and was offered tea, which he sipped slowly while collecting his thoughts.

One of the younger girls approached him and said, "She like you," pointing to his masseuse who had also joined the scene by then. Ray had gotten used to getting compliments, so instead of being at a loss of words, reciprocated by saying, "She very nice too."

The girl continued and said, "She want drink with you, maybe you go to Khaosan Road," to which the woman nodded approvingly while Ray choked on his tea.

"Umm, I have appointment for dinner," he mumbled feebly. They watched him leave, so instead of heading towards Khaosan he made his way back to Shanti Lodge. "Perhaps for the better I suppose as I have an early flight," he reasoned to himself.

He went back, ordered a big meal and as usual there was a group of travellers there with whom he had a nice conversation. Then he bid the staff girls farewell, who asked him to come back soon.

The next morning, he was on his way to Hanoi with Qatar Airways.

Vietnam Halong Bay on the bamboo trail

Ray was feeling nostalgic for Thailand as he took his seat. His first foray into backpacking had gone well, now he felt quite detached from his normal jet-setting business development work and active lifestyle. Instead he had gone into carpe-diem[10] mode and was living without a planned itinerary, rather relying on advice he got from fellow travellers on places to visit, eat and sleep. He was pleased with that development on the other hand he was missing Hilary in particular.

For a change to his previous flights, Ray was sitting next to a bloke this time. He looked Southern European with his dark hair and thick eyebrows. He was a bit dishevelled and looked like he had been on a long flight. Ray smiled at him and inquired, "Long flight?"

"Oef oui, I started in Paris to Qatar, then Bangkok, now finalement to Vietnam."

"Ah, you're French?"

"Yes, excusez-moi, my English is not very good when I am tired."

"Pas de problème, je parle un peu de français puis tu peux essayez mais c'étais longtemps que je l'ai pratiqué."[11]

"Merci, if I am stuck I will try French. What's your name?"

"I am Ray, nice to meet you. And you?"

"Yann, nice to meet you too. Are you Thai?"

---

[10]   Seize the day
[11]   No worries, I speak a bit of French so you could try but it's been a long time since I've practiced it.

Ray smiled and said, "No, I am from India originally, but I live in the Netherlands. Now I am backpacking on my own through South East Asia."

"Excellent! For long?"

"I've been on the road for slightly more than a month now, first in Thailand, now my second country onto Vietnam."

"Where all you plan to go?"

"Hmm, initially I had started with the intention to travel to all countries in the region, but I am taking it slower and staying longer at a place, so I think Vietnam and Cambodia and then maybe either Laos or Bali or perhaps to India, relax at my parents. What is your route?"

"Just Vietnam . . . I always wanted to go to Indo-Chine, as you know it was occupied by French, my first time outside Europe but I only have three weeks vacation."

"Ah yes of course. Travelling alone?"

"Oui, I hope to meet people travelling, is it difficult?" Yann paused and added, "You stay in hostels to meet people?"

"So far I have met people in flights, buses, trains, hostels and everywhere in general. In fact I am thinking of staying in hotels in Vietnam, I understand it's is cheaper than in Thailand. My budget is ten euro's a night so if I can get a room for the price, I think I will choose the comfort of privacy."

Ray realized while speaking that his knowledge of backpacking had shot up considerably in a month.

"C'est cool! Did you reserve a hotel?"

"Nah, I just go to the area recommended by Lonely Planet and ask and see a few accommodations; if it's clean I take it. What about you?"

"Normally in Europe I go to the tourist centre and go to a hostel in the centre."

"Think it'll be somewhat different in Vietnam," said Ray with a wink.

"Do you have a route in mind?"

"Hmm, approximately . . . I plan to ask fellow travellers on the spot itself. What about you?"

"One of my friends did this trip last year, I plan travel along the coast, first to Hanoi and Halong Bay, then to Hue in the centre of Vietnam, then Hoi An, Nha Trang, Mui Ne and finally through the mountains to Saigon, from there I have a flight back to Hanoi and then I have to go back to France."

"Sounds like a good route, I'll probably also do most of the places you mentioned."

Ray didn't know whether it was his desire to stay away from girls for the time-being or whether it was the friendly countenance of Yann which prompted him to say, "Perhaps we could travel a bit together?"

"Sure, excellent!"

"You wouldn't mind hotel rooms or do you really want to stay in a hostel dorm? I tend to snore sometimes so it's perhaps nicer to have own rooms than a dorm."

"Pas de problèmes, I am getting a bit old for hostels and party all the time."

"Yeah, I have noticed a few types of backpackers, the ones there for the party, some for serious sight-seeing only, some on the quest to find themselves, some the first time travelling . . ." trailed Ray.

"And what type are you?"

"I guess the oddball backpacker, as though I've travelled a lot, it is my first time backpacking for a long duration."

They arrived at the Hanoi International airport in the afternoon. Ray wondered how his visa procedure would go as he had booked the eVisa online. It was not exactly an electronic Visa, rather a sort of pre-approval which would enable him to obtain the visa on arrival at the International airport. He was expecting a bureaucratic long-wait, however to his pleasant surprise it just turned out to be an efficient procedure. Yann had already a visa he had got in France.

Coming outside the customs zone, the differences were even more apparent. He had left Bangkok at thirty degrees Celsius; here it was quite cold in comparison, perhaps ten degrees or so. It was also quite overcast, grey and cold. He quickly put on the lone pullover he was carrying. There was an 'Information Office' to which they swayed into. It was quickly apparent to Ray that it was just a private agency selling very expensive hotels and tours and working in conjunction with the taxi drivers.

The boys hastily went outside the terminal to get the Vietnam airlines bus which would take them to the centre, as mentioned on the Lonely Planet guide. The only problem was that once they were outside, every bus they looked at, claimed to be the original Vietnam Airlines Bus.

Ray laughed and said, "In Thailand, they are charming and coax you into buying, here the accent seems to be on the hoax." He spotted a policeman and asked him which one was the real one. The policeman, a scowling small man replete in a khaki uniform and helmet, pointed to a small non descriptive bus.

"But of course, the one you would least expect," said Yann.

Midway through the bus-ride, a tout boarded the bus and started showing photos of his hotel. At ten dollars per room per night, it seemed like a good deal, so the boys decided to take a look and alighted from the bus. It is right in the old-city and clean, so they took a chance, moreover dusk was starting to fall.

When they returned to the lobby to register, the tout turned out to be the owner and also ran a tour-service. He started cross selling a Halong-Bay special tour. His demeanour suddenly transformed from a smile to a scowl when the boys declined.

True to his Gaulic temper, Yann was ready to walk away to another hotel.

"Long journey my friend, let us refresh and we discuss later," said Ray to the owner trying to diffuse the situation. 'Again so different to Thailand', he thought. He figured that this as something to do with history, after all, the Vietnamese had been occupied by foreigners (first the Chinese, then French, then the Americans) and had survived. There was this unmistakable pride in their behaviour.

"I desperately need some sleep!" exclaimed Yann. "Just for a few hours, perhaps we could meet later in the evening?"

"Sure; I'll saunter around town."

The hotel was located in the middle of the old district; Ray got a map from the hotel and started on his way. The old quarter befitted the image of Asia from afar, small bustling streets full of vendors and mostly pedestrians on the streets with the occasional motorbike whizzing past. There were hawkers cooking up a heady noodle-soup (Pho) and the unmistakable smell of oriental cooking, herbs and fish-sauces. Ray passed the colonial Church built by the French; however the absence of maintenance had blackened this imposing originally white-washed church.

Church in Hanoi

'The European colonists imposed their religion on the colonies to stamp their authority on the local,' thought Ray as he walked further. Next there were shops selling old communist propaganda posters to groups of American tourists. Ray smiled at the thought of how the world changes in a couple of decades.

He suddenly came across a shop selling antique watches and there was a watchmaker repairing watches. There were Cartier's and Omega's and the old man smiled at Ray and invited him to take a look. Ray had always had a fascination for watches and though he abhorred fake ones, these seemed genuine in their depleted state. He considered that probably without proper Internet access to comparative websites, this old man didn't probably know the value of the gems he was holding. He asked for the price of a couple of models.

The negotiations went with the help of a calculator, the old man typed in the number and said dollar to emphasize that these were not in dongs.

Ray tried on a few models and then his eye fell on a Patek Philippe and he decided to buy it. He had not changed to the local currency yet, so paid in dollars. Happily he made his way back to the hotel and showed his new acquisition to the local staff.

"How much you pay, twenty dollars?" asked one of them helpfully.

"Umm, a bit more," panic bells ringing in his head. "Where can I get some local money?"

"Come, I take you on motorcycle to 'E en seth' cash machine"

"Ok, thanks," Ray wondered what it was but he was feeling adventurous after his antique buy.

The machine of ANZ bank, as it turned out, was on the road around the lake in the old quarter. It was amazing to see this liquid heart in the middle of the bustle of the traffic around. Ray was reminded of the lake in Hamburg, which also adorned the centre of the city.

Soon, Ray was a millionaire in dongs, the local currency. No wonder the shop-keepers quoted prices in dollars. His mind was still on the veracity of the watch when he arrived back at the hotel, so he decided to go back to the shop. This time, the old man was sitting with a boy who was in his twenties, both sipping a cup of tea.

"Can I help you?" asked the boy in perfect English.

The usage of English dawned Ray to the fact that his assumption about them not knowing the value of these 'antiques' was not exactly apposite. He realized that he had been duped and wanted to return the watch. He felt anger rising and said, "Look I just bought it and I want to return it because it's a fake!"

The amiable old man suddenly turned hostile and a group gathered around Ray. His anger was replaced by a fear; Ray decided to back down and take his loss, after all, he had bought thinking it was an under-prized antique. An experience richer and ninety dollars poorer, he felt resentment rising against this country he had just landed in but he had no choice but to make his way back to the hotel. He looked irritated at the vendors trying to approach him and decided, it would be wise to take a warm shower in order to cool down. He was mostly angry at himself for falling for the scam.

After getting refreshed, he went to see if Yann was awake and he was, so the boys ventured out. Ray needed a jacket of sorts, 'If it was cold in Hanoi, it would be freezing in Halong Bay he reckoned.' They reached a main street and saw some shops on the other side of the road; the only challenge ahead was to negotiate the way to cross the street. Cars and motors of all shapes and sizes were zigzagging past and while there were traffic-lights, not everybody seemed to follow them.

The boys made a run for it when the traffic had briefly ebbed. It was a dangerous strategy; a motor came very close to hitting Ray.

"Merde[12]!," said Ray, trying his best in French slang.

"Ah no, if you say Merde, you should also say alors," corrected Yann.

"Merde alors!" Ray repeated with passion.

They paused to examine how the locals were crossing the streets and actually the strategy was entirely opposite to the one just followed. The locals would cross at a very slow pace between the vehicles, while looking at the drivers. The drivers in turn would zigzag past the pedestrians crossing and try not to hit them. It seemed to work like rhythmic gymnastics . . .

Ray bought a warm beige jacket and thereafter the boys went scouting for food. The narrow streets were teeming with people,

---

[12]   Shit!

jostling for bargains from the various street vendors selling fake Gucci's and Louis Vuitton's.

"There's another difference to Thailand, this is positive here that they don't chase you to buy their stuff," said Ray, trying to brush off his earlier duped transaction. He did not mention it to Yann, his pride was hurt and he felt a bit stupid. He resolved not to buy seemingly underpriced great-buys in the future. As someone said, if something was too good to be true, it probably was not (true).

The group of young attractive girls was passing and Yann asked them for a recommendation to eat well. The girls led the boys to a restaurant which was supposedly the place to be for locals too. Yann asked if they would join them now or later, the girls giggled and said there were on the way home.

"You're quite fluid with the ladies eh?" said Ray after the boys had been seated in the restaurant.

"No no, I was being polite."

They didn't know what to order, so just pointed at what the group at the next table was eating. It turned out to be delicious grilled fish, which the boys gobbled down at will for they were hungry.

"Shall we book a tour of Halong Bay?"

"Yes, I've heard that it's very nice."

When the boys were back in the hotel, the owner put up his best behaviour and suggested that they leave for Halong Bay the next morning as it was predicted to be clearer weather.

"Halong Bay better than Hanoi when clear weather," he said.

"What do you think Yann?"

"Well, why not?"

Ray had read on the Lonely Planet that it was best not to go with the cheapest package as the quality of the boats varied extremely. They chose a two nights, three days package which would include a night on the boat and a night on Cat Ba Island.

"So, bonne nuit, it's gonna be a early day tomorrow."

Ray must have been exhausted, as he was in deep slumber as soon as he hit the sack. It was pretty cold when he woke up the next morning. Without central heating it seemed colder than the winters back home. He gingerly took a shower and went out of his room for breakfast where he was greeted by a beaming Yann, who was enjoying some eggs and baguette.

"They make proper bread here, a legacy we left behind."

"Ah, let me get that too," said Ray. "Man, it's cold eh?"

"Umm, its okay for me, I just came from cold Europe. I think you have been out in the Sun too long."

They were picked up by a small bus; the group seemed quite diverse in terms of nationalities. Yann picked up a conversation with two American girls, both of whom were professional photographers, a brunette and a red-head.

"What do you photograph?" Ray asked the red-head. He had always fancied redheads.

"We're food and drinks photographers."

"Wow really, is that a specialist trade? So you make ordinary food look delicious and appetizing. For instance the hamburgers, they aren't half as good as in real-life eh?"

"Well actually, I just do the photo, there's a food styling specialist who arranges the food. Same for drinks."

"I am amazed that these are professions you can make a living off. The Netherlands is quite small; I don't think you can make a sustainable income of such trades."

"You'll be surprised. Well, some are further than the others. Sometimes I need to shoot a wedding when the assignments are at low ebb. Besides I think you should do you like," she paused and added, "Make a job out of your hobby and you'll never have to work again for the rest of your life."

"True, but there are so many things I like; besides I think to earn the same amount of money as a photographer as I do now, I would have to work shit-loads and it wouldn't be as much fun."

"So what do you do now?"

"I am a business development executive working in an IT company."

"Sounds very grave," she said with a wink and then continued, "Do you enjoy it?"

"Well yes. I see a job also as a means to pay the bills and other things, such as travel," he said waving his hands in a circle to emphasis the travelling. "Every job has good and bad parts, you gotta find one with enough good parts no?"

"Sure, I love the freedom in my job; can take off on a three weeks vacation like this."

"Sounds good, I am on a half-year sabbatical," Ray said triumphantly.

"You win," she said bowing slightly in mockery.

It was about a four hour drive in the small rickety bus to Halong Bay and Ray was anxious about the quality of the boat. From the shore, they took a small boat to their abode for the coming days. Then, they were transferred to a sailing vessel, these were called 'junks' explained the guide; the name derived from an old Chinese design sailing ship. The junk was made almost entirely of wood, seemed quite sturdy and had a sail that was flattened though. It had seen a lot of voyages it seemed from the worn look it bore. The ambience was quite charming with a small bar, lanterns hanging on the walls and an open upper deck for viewing the great beyond.

Junk Boat

The boys went to drop their stuff in the cabin and it was a quaint old-style room replete with old lamps, a small bathroom and perhaps most importantly, a heating system.

Cabin in Junk boat

"Very cosy eh?" said Ray.

"It is very romantic, maybe we should change room-partners," replied Yann with a wink.

"Oh, I am off girls for the time-being."

"Ouch, sounds like a bad break-up happened. So, no 'sedacteur' act for you tonight!"

"Well, not a bad-break-up or so, but I dunno perhaps it's nice to just travel with without the complications of romance involved."

"Who was taking about romance," said Yann with a laugh.

"True true, well, if you are getting lucky, I'll be happy to change rooms, let me know."

They returned to the main deck and were seated for a sumptuous lunch consisting of assorted seafood, including calamari, which was a particular favourite of Ray. The group was quite jovial; it comprised American, French, Canadian, Russian, Argentinean and Singaporean nationalities. The boat had begun sailing and soon they were on the way to the Bay. It was cold and somewhat misty, though they could see quite far in the horizon.

They were taken to one of the several hundred islands in the Bay; this one housed the so-called 'Amazing cave'. It was a steep climb to reach the cave which then afforded a panoramic view of the Bay. The cave itself had two chambers, the outer one being somewhat like wide waiting area of a theatre. In the other chamber, stalactites hung from the roofs in all shapes and designs.

"Look at crocodile; look at dragon . . ." the guide kept pointing to the various shapes on the route.

The cave was brilliantly illuminated with the walls reflecting hues of red, orange, green and blue. It was quite magnificent, probably the most voluminous Ray had seen. The colours seemed surreal and it was difficult to make out which ones were real and which artificially lighted. In the far corner, there was natural blue skylight and Ray closed his eyes and imagined a girl walking up a flight of stairs into the external world.

Amazing cave in Halong Bay

They went outside and vendors were selling cigarettes and cheap rice-vodka, the latter which Yann proceeded to haggle and buy. The guide warned that the boat owners would not like it as they wanted their guests to buy drinks from the bar. Yann and the American girls ignored that warning while Ray, not seeking confrontation, abstained, he sensed disconcert on the guide's face and smiled at him.

"Problem?" enquired Ray.

"I also guest on boat," said the guide. "They no like if you bring own alcohol to boat."

True to his prediction, the boat owners were not amused with the cheap rice vodka bottles and insisted that these be taken away or to pay a surcharge for bringing on board. They pointed to a terms & conditions list on the board which stated amongst other things that own alcohol may not be carried on board.

"Nobody said that when we were booking the trip," shouted the American brunette.

The staff shouted back incomprehensively and the situation seemed to be escalating.

"There's not much you can do I am afraid, we're in the Bay and I think their word is King here," said Ray to the quarrelling tourists.

Somehow those words seemed to have a calming effect and they reluctantly handed over their bottles.

"Well, I've heard that South Vietnam is more like Thailand, I hope it gets better there!" said Ray to Yann once they had settled down.

"You liked it more there?"

"I think so, the people are friendlier, while here they seem to bear a grudge towards tourists and everything seems to be centred on the hoax here."

It was getting darker and they moved to the upper deck from where Halong Bay looked at its best; with the slight mist but long visibility, it was an eerie mix like a scene from a ghost-movie.

"Breathtaking eh?"

View of Halong Bay

They anchored for the night in the bay amongst other boats. Soon moods were uplifted as conversation started ebbing in the group. Dinner was served and it was again quite nice sea-fare. Yann and the American girls decided to pay the surcharge and buy back the vodka bottle and soon drinks were flowing. Ray spied a bottle of Grand Marnier in the junk's make-shift bar; it was his favourite after-dinner liquor and the boat-owner was quite pleased when he ordered it.

Entertainment consisted of Karaoke music and pretty soon all the group were either singing along or dancing to the many classics in the collection. Yann and Ray were the only ones in the with a three-day tour; the other leaving back for Hanoi the next day as they just had the two-day version. The boys were told that they would be picked up early in the morning and transferred to another boat.

The next song on play was, "Where did you come from where did you go?" Yann was from Bretagne in France and that region had Gaelic roots. He aptly demonstrated the Gaelic / Irish dance for the song.

Everyone joined, including the boat staff and they made an amazing amount of noise which was a stark contrast to the eerie silence outside. Some songs and dances later, Ray retired to the cabin at a wee hour, tired but exuberant while some of the die-hards including Yann still partied on. The cabin was nice and warm, he was glad they'd taken the slightly more expensive tour. He slept soundly and was only woken up by the alarm next morning.

A quick shower and packing later, Ray joined the guide for a breakfast and coffee in the main while Yann got ready in the cabin. The guide was looking much more cheerful now that the confrontation the previous evening had not escalated into real trouble.

"Tough life eh?" inquired Ray

"Yes. Tour operator book, no give information, guide gets trouble. I work all the time, during holiday, work on weekend, all the time."

"Perhaps work abroad?"

The guide smiled and said, "My family is here, we survivors. Lots of Vietnamese leave from South Vietnam to US after war. They come back now because better here. We are bamboo nation!"

"Bamboo?"

"Yes, we are flexible like bamboo and can bend, but united we are strong like bamboo together."

Ray smiled and felt respect for this folk who had survived some thousand years of Chinese occupation and thereafter French and American and always persevered in the end.

"Tell me, why do so many people hoax around here?"

"What is hoax?"

"Hmm, example you buy water at same place, but they ask you different price the next day, or I give money and for change they give back ten thousand dong note instead of hundred thousand notes thinking I will not notice. That is hoaxing."

"It is changing. Earlier, the government had propaganda that tourists were imperialists with a lot of money so you should take as much from them as possible."

"Wow . . . and now?"

"They realize that tourist go back to Thailand but not come back here, so bad for long-term business. Bamboo nation, we change, now government tell us to be polite to tourists and be kind." He paused and asked, "You don't like it here?"

"Well I am beginning to warm up to the ways. I loved Halong Bay."

Yann joined them in the meanwhile for a coffee and exclaimed, "Oooh, my head!"

"The rice vodka was potent eh?"

"Oef yes. You have no effect?"

"Ah I stayed put with the Grand Marnier."

"So you paid then five dollars for every glass instead of drinking the ten dollar vodka! You don't like confrontation do you?"

"Well I think they were happy that someone was at least having drinks from them so they gave me large servings. Plus I really like Grand Marnier, was so happy to see it yesterday, so far I'd only had cheap rum in my travels."

"Bien sur[13]."

"Did you have a nice time? Any luck with the ladies?"

"It was great; we didn't really stay very long after you left. No luck, they were actually all settled girls. By the way, you snore like a King!"

"Oops sorry, did you have troubles falling asleep?"

"Ah non, I sleep like a rock. But I heard you; it was easy to find the room from the corridor," said Yann with a big smile.

After breakfast, they were picked up by a small boat which brought them to another Junk-vessel. The guests on that boat were just waking up when the boys arrived.

The tour packages seemed to be very modular, how the Junk and tour operators communicated and split the money in the absence of IT systems was probably another bamboo-like flexible function thought Ray.

"Ahoy," said one of the blokes on the new junk. "From where are you guys landing from?"

"That boat over there," said Ray pointing to their previous night's residence.

---

[13]   Of course

"Oh man, from the party boat? You guys were having a blast last night! We could see the lights and hear you even from here."

"Really?"

"It seemed like the scene from the Titanic before they sank. Only you didn't."

"You should've seen my friend's Gaelic dance," said Ray pointing to Yann. What did you guys do then?"

"Hmmm, we played some cards; actually it's quite a boring group, they just went to sleep."

"And now you're all going to Cat Ba Island I suppose."

"Yeah mate, you have the right boat."

"Yes, Cat Ba, here we come!"

"Ssshh," said Yann grasping his head.

Onto warmer pastures

The new boat was hosting a much smaller group; there was an English twosome, two Aussi lads and an American couple; the male being one of oriental parentage and the girl an all-American blond. Yann and Ray were offered breakfast by the boat crew. This boat crew seemed to be more laid-back than the previous one as they offered the fresh arrival some tea and breakfast.

"You guys travelling together?" asked Aussi bloke one.

Yann and Ray exchanged a glance and nodded in the affirmative, "Well, we met on the flight and have been on the road since a couple of days."

"Well, you are on water actually," offered Aussi bloke two.

"Thanks mate for the clarification," said Ray sarcastically. He was not much of a morning person.

Cat Ba was the largest of the two thousand odd islands on Halong Bay, quite full of tropical vegetation. As this boat docked, the group was swarmed with people selling all sorts of wares, also pearls. 'Who would want to buy pearls early in the morning?' thought Ray.

The first item on the agenda was a National Park and there were two choices, either to climb up a hill or to do a cycle-tour at a leisurely pace.

"So, shall we take it easy?" queried Ray to Yann.

"C'mon, it's a chance to sweat out the alcohol from yesterday," egged Yann.

Hill-climb it was thus, actually the entire group decided for it. They were led by a small lady who was walking on loafers with a very flat sole. All the macho men, replete with their special walking shoes, tried to keep up with her in but soon found the pace to be extremely rapid. Ray brought up the rear of the group, panting and painfully reminded of his condition or rather the lack of it.

"Lazy man," said the old lady guide laughing at him.

"Hey, I am not lazy, I am doing it ain't I?"

"Don't worry," said the American girl and added helpfully, "I run cross country so am more used to this."

"And I jog every week and my boyfriend runs the Marathon," said the English bird.

"Ah, of all company's to seek, a decade younger blokes and endurance women," muttered Ray as he thought of Goldratt's theory of constraints and the weakest link.

"Do you sport?" asked Yann.

"Yes, a lot, but more explosive sports and not endurance sports," panted Ray.

They eventually reached the top and it was well worth the view. They could see the other hills from a panoramic view and it looked mystical in the early morning mist.

View from top of Cat Ba island hill

After a brief rest, they made their way down, by a different route than they had climbed it, Ray was glad to have persevered till the summit. He felt satisfied at having accomplished the task to reaching the top and celebrating on the way down with a little Tarzan-like swing with a vine; only to hit his knee against a rock on the down swing.

Swinging like Tarzan

"You 'urt?" asked Yann.

"Only my pride," answered Ray though he could feel the pain in his knee.

They reached the base, had a drink and were then propped back into the bus. The group was dropped off at different hotels; it had to do with the packages they had taken. Yann and Ray were dropped at the same hotel at the American couple. It was a lovely hotel, the best for Ray on this tour, with a balcony gazing into the hills; but the highlight was the shower with a rainfall shower-cap. Ray took a long and warm shower and then dozed off; it had been a hectic and long day.

It was getting slightly dark when he awoke; momentarily disoriented; then he saw Yann deep in slumber in the other bed. Ray changed and went outside to the balcony. The early evening air was pleasant and while he was standing and enjoying the view, Yann woke up too and joined him.

"C'est le bon vivre quoi?"[14] said Ray.

"Absolutement. Very different from daily life, it'll be difficult to go back to work for you no?"

"I dunno, not thinking about it at all. I must say that the daily life seems very far away now. Maybe I'll become a traveller, going from place to place."

"Like a bum, as they said in Pulp Fiction," grinned Yann.

"You like English movies?"

"Of course, what do you think; we French only watch French movies?"

"Well you have a reputation . . ."

"That's from our politicians."

"Always good to blame the politicians . . . So, did you have some luck with the American girls yesterday?"

"Ah no, they were settled girls, we danced wildly, but further nothing. I usually end up with blond girls and these were brunettes, replied Yann with a wink and then asked, "You're not into the chasing game?"

"Well, I do love the game sometimes actually, but sort of recovering and am not exactly in the mood."

"Recovering from a bad break-up?"

"Ahh, sort of, long story actually . . . but I met this quite nice girl on the flight to Thailand but she disappeared after a few days to the Islands and then I met another girl with whom I had a very romantic time but she's also gone back now."

---

14   It's the good life eh?

"So what's the problem?"

"Umm, I dunno to be very honest. The problem is not in attracting girls I think that I manage well. However it's never stuck in the long-term. My relations have varied from three weeks, three months, and six months with one maximum lasting two years."

"Maybe you are approaching it wrong. I do not think much of the long term and just get into something. Sometimes it works out to something longer."

"I think I am scared to grow old alone but perhaps even more scared to grow old with the wrong person."

"Come on, you are still young. Are you really conscious of your age?"

"Well, I am not getting any younger and there will come a time when I cannot attract girls anymore . . ."

"Till that time, enjoy and get laid as much as you can!"

"You do know the expression, men want to get laid and end up getting married and women want to get married and end up getting laid," Ray said with a big smile.

"Cheers to that!"

They changed for the evening and went for dinner at the hotel; which was included in the tour price. The American couple was also there in the restaurant and they waved over to the boys to join them. They introduced themselves as Daisy and Scott.

"Did you guys go to the Monkey beach?" asked Scott.

"Nah, we were knocked-out from the partying yesterday," said Ray.

"Ah yes, of course, the party boat," said Daisy with a wink.

"Yeah, we had quite a lot of booze," said Yann with a grin beaming from ear to ear.

". . . and I am just getting old," said Ray, "Didn't you drink on your boat?"

"He can't really handle much alcohol," grinned Daisy pointing at Scott.

"Asians make cheap dates actually as we can't take much alcohol. The exceptions are the Filipino's, we call them the Mexicans of this region as they have mixed Spanish blood," said Scott with mischief in his eyes.

"So, are you Vietnamese origin?" asked Ray.

"Yes, my parents are from here, though from South Vietnam. They migrated to the US after the war. We are here on out honeymoon trip, first time here for me."

"Feels like a home-coming?"

"He has a phobia of infections. Poor thing, he has to wash his hands at every opportunity," said Daisy and stroked Scott's thick Asian hair.

"Like the guy from 'As good as it gets." Yann seemed to be into his American films.

'It takes all kinds to make this world,' thought Ray. He was also a bit of a cleanliness freak, though to a lesser extent than Scott.

Dinner was excellent, consisting of Noodle soup, fresh-fried fish, chicken and beef, all with hints of exotic spices; served with rice and fried banana as dessert. It was so good that the eaters enjoyed their food in silence, only broken by the occasional 'ummm'.

After dinner, Daisy suggested going shopping for pearl accessories. Her in-laws had educated her that the pearl quality versus price was excellent here.

"Actually not a bad idea to buy pearl presents, small and easy to carry and the girls will love it," said Yann.

They all went down to the sea-front; it was a stark contrast to the bustle of Hanoi. Vendors here were sparse and scattered around selling their wares to the odd tourist scouting for pearls.

Ray bought an assortment of earrings and necklaces for his sister, mother and girlfriend's to be; Yann, who had a larger budget and a shorter time to carry around his backpack, bought even more. Daisy of course, outdid them all.

Morning came and the trip back to Hanoi was uneventful; the boys decided on the way to stay a couple of nights more in Hanoi and see the sights.

Hanoi was much smaller than Bangkok, so they covered the most places by foot, resulting in aching and weary legs. They saw a variety of colonial style houses, which now were the site of foreign embassies. The lake in the middle of the old city-centre was the highlight, as it provided a serene setting against the backdrop of scooters whizzing past the periphery. Ray confided in Yann about his 'antique watch' transaction before they had left for Halong Bay.

Instead of laughing as Ray expected, Yann told Ray about the time that he was duped in London into buying an imitation perfume.

"If something seems too good to be true, it probably is not eh?" quipped Yann.

"Good decisions come from experience and experience comes from bad decisions," quoted Ray.

They both laughed wholeheartedly.

There was of course the customary visit to Ho Chi Minh's resting place. Ho had asked to be cremated; however the folk embalmed him and made a mausoleum. It was however closed on the day of their visit due to some official function, so the guys just observed the huge building and instead spent time in the gardens, which had immaculate bonsai trees.

Bonsai trees in Hanoi

Thereafter Yann wanted to go to the war museum; however Ray declined to accompany him, he knew that it would depress him;

having had the experience in Kanchanaburi in Thailand. Instead he sauntered through the street of Hanoi and drank his favourite Vietnamese coffee, thick black fluid on top of sweet condensed milk. In contrast to how others drank it, Ray would not mix the two; rather enjoy the slightly bitter taste of good coffee followed by the sweetness of the milk. The latter reminded him of his childhood days when his grandmother would make him toast topped with dripping sweet condensed milk.

The boys met up in the evening and in order to recover from all the walking, they went for a massage, the Vietnamese variant being much more of the relaxing sort rather than the yoga-style Thai massage.

"Funnily enough they expect a big tip here in this socialist country as opposed to Thailand," remarked Ray to Yann as they paid.

"How do you know?"

"Well, she told quite that she wanted a big tip," said Ray laughing.

"It's so great to travel widely to experience these differences in a short while. Other things you have noticed?"

"Well, the street food here is mostly limited to Noodle-soup whereas in Thailand there's a big choice and there's no Facebook here, it's blocked by the government."

"I don't miss it."

"Normally I wouldn't either, but I was corresponding with my vacation love through it."

"So, we'll find you a way at an Internet café."

They went to one and Yann was an adept IT guy, so after some searching on the net, found a proxy server to bypass the controls.

Ray logged on expectantly, however there was just a short-note from Hilary. He used the occasion to upload his photos.

"So, nice love letter?"

"Hmmm, no . . . Just a short note, she was busy with work et al."

"Well, there are more fish in the pond."

"True . . . Let's move to warmer pastures."

"Let's do it."

The boys bought a so-called open-bus ticket from Hanoi all the way to Saigon in the Deep South, which meant that they could hop onto inter-city busses all the way along the coast.

The first of the bus trip was from Hanoi to Hue; the latter being the spiritual capital of the country. The night bus was quite a lower standard than the ones Ray had used in Thailand. He could not sit entirely upright, as there were two levels of seats, one above the other. His feet needed to go into a small hole and he could put small things (like shoes) in a small cabinet with a lid under the head.

Vietnam sleeper bus

Ray chose the ground level while Yann took the upper berth, while muttering 'merde alors' due to his obvious discomfort in this environment. The places across the aisle were taken by two backpacker girls, a Hungarian and a French one, in the ground and upper berth respectively. The conversation turned to French in the upper berths while the Hungarian and Dutch-Indian below tried their best to understand.

The Hungarian girl, Maria, remarked that she preferred the lower seats as she could put her stuff around. Ray agreed and added, "I would be a bit scared of falling down from the narrow seats."

"Me too, good selection!"

Their temporary joy was however quite short-lived as the bus started picking up 'local' passengers without a reservation who were happy just to sit on the floor on the aisles and soon the entire bus was packed full and smelling of a dizzy combination of sweat and shoes.

"My friend had warned me about this happening as it is around the Chinese New Year and people travel back to their families in the villages," said Maria.

The frayed tempers of the passengers with reserved seats were in stark contrast to the ones sitting huddled between with faces bearing no countenance at all. The roads were quite bumpy, so the busses did not make much speed either.

Ray tried sleeping but somehow the combination of smell, bouncy roads and chatty passengers was a bit too much. He was glad when after a couple of hours the bus did the customary stop at a touristy place, replete with shops and bright lights. He alighted and got chatting with a pair of Dutch girls from another bus, one extremely tall and one of Ray's posture, both quite blond and tanned. 'Yann would have been happy', thought Ray, but Yann was dozing peacefully in his upper seat. The smaller of the two was quite to Ray's liking and she had a very cute Southern Netherlands (Brabantse) accent. They were also heading south.

"Tot ziens misschien"[15] they said as they parted.

Ray got some semblance of sleep this time and a rambling twelve to thirteen hours later, they were dropped off in Hue.

Hue (pronounced Who-eh) was much warmer, but also much rainier. So far, Ray had been lucky to avoid rain in this trip. South-East Asia had two seasons more or less, dry and wet and was by and large warm all the time (except North Vietnam). At the bus-station they were accosted by various touts; Ray was only too familiar with the routine. The guys took the first option, consisting of spacious rooms and within their budget. The girls wanted to explore some more options, so they went away and arranged to meet later.

"Men are easier to travel with eh?" remarked Yann.

---

[15]   Till we see each other perhaps

"Certainly! I think you should spend more time in discovering the place rather than discovering the hotels and hostels. Though I guess some people like the sport of finding cheaper places."

After freshening up and downing some of the delicious omnipresent Pho (noodle-soup), the boys walked to the citadel. Called Kinh Thanh, it was a city in itself in the ancient times. There was a moat all around the outer walls and the boys decided to take a round. They had ponchos and it was put to good use in the rain. Perhaps due to the rain, there were not many tourists around and they could take time to explore this disintegrating treasure without having to negotiate their way through hordes of people. There was an inner citadel within a citadel. Walking inside felt like a trip back to ancient times with ornate gardens and grand halls used for ceremonies; reflecting the grandeur of the bygone days. They walked for a few hours, rain not deterring the resolve of the boys to experience the surreal and serene ambience of this ancient capital. The serenity was however broken by the sight of tanks lined up. These probably confiscated American tanks were a show of nationalistic pride and propaganda. The American had initially landed via the nearby city of Danang to help the South against the North. The nearby Ben Hai River served as the dividing line between North and South Vietnam.

In the evening they found a little restaurant run by a family of three generations, the grandmother being the cook, the mother the overall manager and the daughter waiting of the customers. The boys got chatting with a Singaporean couple sitting in the adjacent table. When the starter-soup came, Ray remarked that somehow the soup in restaurants never matched up to the ones on the street.

"Ah, that's because they never clean the big pots used for serving in the street," explained the man from Singapore.

"What do you mean?"

"Well, they just add more ingredients and boiling water everyday, so that adds to the taste."

Ray could feel his disgust coming up, though realized that he had not got a stomach upset in Vietnam.

"Remind me never to have any more noodle soup on the street!"

"It's a pity that it has raining so much, could you recommend something to do around here?" asked Yann of the Singaporeans.

"We took a boat trip around the sites, it's quite good, lunch included and the boat is covered so even with rain you are dry."

Hue was replete with museums and mausoleums; so the boys decided to take the organized tour the next day.

"You enjoying the trip so far?" asked Ray to Yann as they made their way to the hotel.

"Of course; though I had expected more warm and less rain. And you?"

"The same! You're a good travel buddy."

"Yes, we seem to have similar tastes and combination of spending the day . . ."

"A bit of sight-seeing and chilling, travelling on a budget but not too fussed."

"It's funny; sometimes I feel we have known each other for a long time."

"In India we have a song which goes sometimes those who were strangers till yesterday are friends for life."

"Cheers to that!"

The next day it was raining again, after having a hearty breakfast in the family restaurant, the boys were picked up to be taken to the boat-trip. It was a small boat with a dragon head structure in the front of the boat. Dragons, as also in the Chinese culture were a symbol of luck in Vietnam. The group was small and included the two girls they had met in the bus-trip. Yann got chatting with his country-mate Lucile, while Ray found himself talking to Maria.

The guide was a funny young man who mixed frivolity with interesting stories. He was quite candid in his views and told stories of the 'puppet' kings under French rule. At one of the museums there was a photo of a famous Vietnamese monk who committed self-immolation at a busy road junction in Saigon. His body had burned but his heart remained intact. Ray was quite interested in knowing the variation of Hindu and Buddhist culture in this country. So he asked about Nirvana, the Hindu concept of being in unison with the supreme universal God and whether it was the same as in Hinduism.

The guide said, "Here anyone can become a Buddha when they have a pure heart and get the ultimate peace of mind without want."

The group was asked whether they wanted to see the tombs of the Kings, they could get entry to all three on the itinerary for a discount price, said the guide. Most of the group decided to take the offer.

The guide attributed the reason for the magnificent resting places to the fact that the puppet kings wanted to have a grand after-life. The three were very different in ambience, one having massive courtyards within the compound; the second very quiet and surrounded by water and terracotta soldiers lining the compound and the third having a very ornate main chamber.

The guide whispered to Ray at the third, "The Americans find it awesome while the French call it kitsch." True to his prediction, the two French were not unduly impressed while the Americans in the group clicked happily.

The day was a heady combination of temples and tombs and Ray suddenly had the feeling that the sights were flashing past.

By the end of the day, he had such a glassy look on his face that Yann remarked, "You look like having a day-dream."

"Umm sorry, it's just that I've been on the road for a while now and absorbing all the new sights, people and culture is taking its toll."

"You want to take it slower?"

"Well perhaps I'll hang around longer in the next city, Hoi An, I've heard it's a charming place and I've got cloth-material which needs to be stitched."

'Ah ok. Lucile was talking about briefly stopping there and thereafter going to two beach town before going to Saigon."

"I think she means Nha Trang and Mue Ne."

"I was thinking of joining her."

"She's quite cute eh? You should! We'll part ways then."

"Umm, no hard feelings?"

"Well, I think people come and go in your life, probably happens with a reason."

"Très sage."

"So let's go to Hoi An tomorrow?"

"Sounds good, let me talk to the girls."

"So, how do you propose to lose Maria?"

"Who's that?"

"Crazy man, it's the Hungarian girl!"

"Well, perhaps you can help, be the wing-man!"

"Nopes mate. Not doing the dirty work, you'll have to figure out with Lucile."

In the evening, they went to their favourite family restaurant together with the girls and had a couple of drinks afterwards. The French pair was getting romantic, so it became a natural parting of ways. Ray bid them goodbye and sauntered to his hotel room.

It was still raining the next morning; Ray hoped it would be better weather in Hoi An, which was some four hours by bus. He went for breakfast and was joined by Yann and Lucile; the romance had apparently further blossomed in the previous night.

"We would like to spend one more day in Hue before heading southwards, to Hoi An and the beaches," said Yann. They were still soaking up the culture, not having been so long on the road as Ray.

"Well mon ami, it was great meeting you. Have fun!" said Ray.

"Maybe we could meet in the South?"

"We'll see, let's sms when we get there."

"Take care mon ami."

Ray made his way to the bus-station and was soon on a picturesque ride to Hoi An.

Moments of respite and reflection

The bus was again a Vietnamese sleeper with the same strange seat contraption as the one from Hanoi to Hue, however of superior quality. Learning from his experience then of 'unreserved' travellers squatting around the ground floor, this time Ray chose an upper berth. Since this was a daytime ride, he could also look out of the window at the surrounding scenery. The view varied between a mountainous territory and the sea against a very steep cliff as the bus made its way along small and curving roads. So although the distance was not that great, it still took some four to five hours to reach Hoi An and it was twilight when they finally reached.

True to the hoax principle, the bus dropped the travellers at a solitary hotel which was away from the main lodging area of the city, so that the travellers could either check-in the hotel or trek to the city-centre.

It was a luxury hotel replete with a swimming pool, probably at par with the superior bus quality. Ray was somewhat tired after the journey and the hotel promised of a shuttle service to a drop-off point in a city-centre, so he decided to engage in negotiations rather than trek with his backpack to the centre. The hotel staff at the reception was very smartly-dressed and Ray had by this time started to look like a worldly backpacker; so they eyed him with some trepidation.

"I want cheapest room," asked Ray who, in his worldly backpacker image, had learnt to omit prepositions and pleasantries.

"We have single at twenty five dollars, special price for you."

"Of course special price," muttered Ray. "My budget is ten dollars," he replied with a smile.

"Oh, we have basement room for twelve dollars, but no breakfast included."

In the end, they settled for that price but with breakfast included. The room was quite luxurious, reminiscent of the one in Cat Ba Island, though of course this time Ray was not sharing with Yann.

Room in Hoi An

The hotel also had bicycles to borrow and like a true adopted-Dutchman, Ray took one to foray into the city-centre. The Netherlands is a very flat country and Ray often used the bike for small commutes.

It was a very pleasant climate and about a kilometre to the ancient city. Reaching it, Ray immediately fell in love with the very picturesque city. Hoi An had been an international trading port dating back a couple of centuries and now deemed an UNESCO world heritage site. The old centre was more or less preserved in its original pristine form. Wooden houses with intricate carving lined the narrow streets and parting two sides of the town was a stream of water, a tributary of the Thu Bon River. Tailor-shops were abundant and Ray smiled thinking of the cloth material he had carried all the way from Thailand. The weather was absolutely marvellous, a cool evening breeze and clear skies. Ray closed his eyes in inner contemplation and was engulfed with a feeling of bien-être[16].

The water-front was lined with an excess of restaurants and cafés, much more than Ray had expected of a small city. He chose a restaurant with a view directly on the water and managed to get a table facing the water. It was dark and the street illumination provided a romantic view of the water and the opposite side of the old town. His bien-être feeling was replaced with a bit of the lonesome and he put up a pensive look. It was perhaps that or perhaps some other reason that an elderly couple came up and inquired whether they could share the table as it was the last one facing the water.

"Sure! Though we'll have to sit side-by-side for all of us to view the water," joked Ray.

"Pardon, could you please repeat? My English is not good," replied the man with a strong French accent.

"Ah, pas de problème, on doit s'asseoir ensemble, ummm, en le meme côté," Ray repeated in his best broken French.

"C'est merveilleux, vous parlez français,"[17] and then proceeded to rattle off a couple of sentences of which Ray only picked up a few words.

"Ah pardon, mais je préfère parler en anglais. C'était longtemps que j'ai pratiqué le français"[18], said Ray; which was not entirely accurate as he would speak once in a while in French with Yann, however he was tired after the long journey and had no desire to make a supreme effort in conversation.

"You travel alone?" asked the lady, her English accent in any case seemed to indicate a better command of the language than her better half.

"Yes and off and on with companions."

"No girlfriend?"

"Ah no."

---

[16]   Well-being
[17]   That's marvellous, you speak French
[18]   I prefer to speak in English, it's been a while since I spoke French

These questions, although having being asked numerous times before, got Ray thinking, 'Am I a loner?', 'Do I have commitment problems?'

He started replying, also to sort out his thoughts, "The thing is, I am travelling for a long time, have half a year off. I like travelling with others, but also like being able to do what I like, stay longer somewhere when I like the place, or leave if I don't like it that much." He paused and added, "Also, I planned this last moment, so not a lot of people can get off vacations for so long."

"So you like being alone?"

"Well no, of course I am scared of growing old alone, but I have a nice life, great friends and family, lots of hobbies and things to do and I don't want to settle with the first best girl who comes along." He realized he was rattling off to strangers, though it felt a bit strange, it also felt easy to do so. "I think I just haven't met the right girl yet . . . do you find it odd then?"

"Ah non non. My daughter is also I think your age and she is also a randonneur, how do you say that in English?"

"Backpacker I think?"

"Yes yes, she loves this region, also because of the French influence and is coming back during the school vacances[19] every year. She is a teacher. When I was her age, I already had two children, but she does not want to settle down."

"I see. Perhaps I am not that odd after all," Ray said with a smile. "I think perhaps she travels a lot, meets a lot of people, changes jobs and such things that people at my age have already done a lot of things much quicker than previous generations."

"Too many choices!"

"Indeed, and short-attention spans! When I was twenty, I did not know what to do with the rest of my life, now I am moving towards forty but I still don't know."

"And so you travel to find out?"

"Yeah, sort of but then you are also travelling no?"

---

[19]   vacations

"Yes, of course, my daughter and a lot of other friends recommended this part of the world."

"Come to think of it, I have indeed met a lot of French in Vietnam."

"It was called Indochine."

"They even have baguette here," said Ray with a smile.

"It's not like the baguette in France," the couple said in unison with Gaelic pride.

Ray had ordered a local specialty with chicken and herbs and it was awesome. The food was getting better compared to the North part of the country along with the climate, he felt. Vietnamese food had a more Chinese influence, that is, more stir-fry and sauces than the Thai one which was more curry based. However compared to Chinese food, it was less greasy and had fresh ingredients.

"Do you like your food?" inquired Ray of the couple.

"Ah oui, c'est bon," said the man. "You like French food?"

"Yes sure. I think of European food I like the French and Spanish the most as they are also with herbs and spices, similar to Indian in certain ways. I read somewhere that taste is formed in the early years."

The good meal later, Ray bid them farewell, managed to find the bicycle and started peddling towards the hotel. It was pitch-dark as soon as he had passed the historic centre; after all, Hoi An was a small city. He was a bit apprehensive being on his own and there was not a soul in sight. On the way, there was a small hut-like bar where the revelries still seemed to be on.

He saw the lights of the hotel in a distance and started peddling faster and reached in a bit of a huff and sweating profusely to which the girls at the reception started giggling. His thoughts from earlier in the evening on why he was alone still rattled him though. Ray considered he had always been a bit different from the groups he hung around with, from his early school-days to university and work. He started recollecting passages; his dear friend Arun from his school and university days had said, "You are a bit of an oddball," or his Mother, "A bit eccentric" or his ex, who called him "Tjonge tjonge" meaning 'boy o boy'. Coupled by his hectic work and plethora of hobbies, it probably made him a difficult catch. 'Something needs to change', mused Ray.

The hotel-room had a bath and Ray decided to take a long one. It helped to sooth the tired body and mind from a long travel day. The room was air-conditioned and Ray was asleep almost as soon as he hit the sack.

✦

The next day was bright and sunny and Ray decided to find a tailor. He had been carrying around the cloth-material all the way from Thailand and was looking forward to relieve the load. He took the complimentary shuttle bus from the hotel to the city-centre, alighting and looking at all the tailor shops around him; he was faced with the choice-stress characteristic of his generation. He was probably looking around with glazed-eyes, as a lady from a shop came out of the shop to him and asked if he was looking for clothes to be made.

"Yes I am looking around," said Ray trying not to commit to her shop.

She said, "You only look ok, come in," grasped him by the arm and tugged him inside.

Back in Europe, there was an image of Asian women being docile, for the umpteenth time Ray thought how different that image was from the reality.

It was a quite neat shop and there were some five women ranging from ages young to old stitching clothes and glancing up with a smile at Ray.

"Are you all tailors?" inquired Ray to the lady who had dragged him in.

"Our tailors work in other place. Here we make fit and last changes. You stay long here?"

"Just came yesterday, so yes the next couple of days."

"Good good, so we can make good fit, you come back next two-three days ok?"

"Ah, I have not yet decided. How much will it cost? I have the material already."

At which point, a somewhat more senior lady, presumably the proprietor stepped in to join the sales pitch, "Here, we have lot of foreigner coming. We ship it for you if you want, all take care."

"I want good price. How much for stitching one shirt? And for one suit?"

"You handsuum man, I give you good price."

South East Asia was such an ego-booster for Ray, by this time he had somewhat got used to receiving unexpected compliments and he recognised it as probably a sales technique.

"How old are you?" she asked.

"What do you think?"

"Twenty eight."

"You charmer you, no I am much older."

"You have wife?"

"Umm no. You have husband?"

"No, I look for husband," she said with a wink. This girl was much more mischievous than others. And so the banter continued till the boss stepped in again to make the deal. The usual negotiation ensued, since Ray had multiple suits and shirts to be made, they agreed on a good unit-price. Ray never really bargained to the bone, as he wanted a win-win deal, also he reasoned he was much better off than the locals so it would be unfair to have a bare-minimum deal.

Next was the fitting part, Ray wanted a streamlined finish for the tailored look. Ready-made suits somehow never fitted him well; while he was too broad for Italian suits around the shoulders; German suit-brands would be roomy and too long for his stature. The ladies came with numerous folders with images of suits in all shapes. Ray browsed through them and pointed at one tentatively, "Is this possible?"

"Of course possible!"

"If fitting good, maybe I make more."

"We give you good price also for cloth."

"Sure."

"You pay us some deposit now?"

His cloth-material and a couple of thousands of dongs lighter, Ray stepped out in the bright-day and decided to explore the cultural part of this UNESCO city. There was a booth selling tickets to the town's historic sights and Ray bought a set, which also included a small guide to the major sights. He started at the Japanese bridge. This several hundred year old bridge was supposedly started in the year of the monkey and completed in the year of the dog of the Vietnamese calendar. Hence there were small deities of both these animals on the respective sides.

On the opposite side of the bridge there were numerous shops selling ready-made clothes. Ray was in the shopping mood, so stopped to buy some. He resolved that if the fitting was good and comfortable, he would give away his old T-shirts to orphanages or so. He normally also donated his old clothes back home, people were always happy to receive his in good condition clothes.

Thereafter he spent the entire day playing the tourist, going from old houses to temples and meandering through the town in general. The food was delicious, even the simple noodle soup had a tang to it and in the evening he ordered the specialty of the town, white-rose, which was shrimp enclosed in white rice-paper and steamed to perfection.

White rose delicacy

The cool breeze next to the river was soothing and he wondered how life would be to live without the hectic of his normal job in a remote part like Hoi An.

'To live without much and without a care in the world. Probably would get absolutely bored after a while,' he muttered to himself.

After dinner he went to a patisserie, which had the most delicious looking cakes but at steep European prices. While he was enjoying his cake on the terrace of the shop, a beggar came up to the tables. Normally it was not his practice to give to beggars, however this man had amputated legs and as he approached, Ray felt a pang of remorse at his blues of being alone. He thought of the expression, 'I had a blue that I had no shoes, until I saw a man who had no feet'. His troubles were so minute compared to this man.

The man's shirt was a bit torn, so Ray instinctively gave him his old T-shirts. The man's face lit up in an instant and he thanked Ray profusely and left. Ray felt tears streaming down his face as emotions got the better of him. He finished his cake slowly and then made his way back to the hotel. He considered how lucky he was to just be normal and healthy. He was of middle-class origins, but had become comfortably well-off in the meantime. He had a lot to be grateful for, were his parting thoughts as he went to sleep.

The next morning he decided to go to the beach, which was some ten kilometres away. Again he took a bicycle and made his way out of the town and into the countryside. On his way, he saw even more tailor and shoe shops. Perhaps they would have been cheaper, but the fitting, the English speaking staff and shipping facilities to Europe of the bigger shops were probably better in their totality to his needs.

The meandering road followed a stream of river for a while as the town changed into villages and the countryside. People were working on farms in typical conical shaped straw hats; it could have been out of a picture postcard. It was sweltering hot and Ray stopped at a local village bar of sorts for a drink. The locals grinned from ear to ear as him as he sipped his tea; as he was the only foreigner there. Thereafter he cycled on and soon he could smell the salty sea. Coconut trees lined the beach with its white, fine sands.

The sea seemed a bit rough, Ray was happy just to roll in the sand under the shadow of a tree. Palm-thatched huts were setup to cater to tourists. The calming sound of the water splashing against the shore coupled with the warm induced Ray to drowse off.

Once awake, he bought a coconut to drink the fresh milk. He was sipping at it when he was approached by a vendor. She was covered top-to-bottom in clothes which made for a stark contrast to the tourists worshipping the Sun God in bare minimum clothes. Ray asked if she was not feeling warm.

"In my country we do not want to be dark. That's why we cover."

"Ah, it's the same in India, the not wanting to be dark part."

"Ok. I have to try to sell you something."

"I understand, but I already have so many things and my backpack is really, really full."

"I have not many sales today, so please buy something from me. Maybe some decoration chopsticks to give to friends?" she persevered.

"Well actually I could use some myself."

Some chopsticks and armbands exchanged hands for some thousands dongs and Ray went back to his reverie. He wanted to change his lifestyle, one step at a time. For starters he decided to buy less branded clothes in favour of local labour produced material. He had a challenging and stressful job though; it also paid for his travels. He wondered whether he could live a simple nomadic life or become a beach-boy.

The afternoon flew by and Ray flitted between day-dreaming and nodding off to sleep in the warm Sun and cool-breeze. Finally it was dusk and he decided to make his way back to Hoi An town. By this time, he knew his way around this charming town like the back of his hand. He decided to stop for a cultural show before heading for dinner. He still had his booklet of coupons which he wanted to use.

There was a dance and music show at six at one of the venues and Ray went for it. It was a small venue and Ray was luckily to have arrived early, as soon the place was crammed to the full with tourists. First there was a music orchestra played by people in traditional attire and that was followed by a dance ensemble. The silk is the dresses matched the silky movement as Ray sat there mesmerized by the performance.

Music and dance show in Hoi An

He was so into the show and still enjoying an after-effect at the end that he was quite startled when somebody tapped him on his back. It was the Hungarian girl from Hue, who had been travelling with the French girl, the latter being presumably now with Yann.

"Hi again," he said.

"You look startled."

"Yeah, sorry, I was in a reverie. Small world eh?"

"Exactly. I came here today from Hue."

"I've been here already since a couple of days. I must say I forgot your name."

"Maria. I forgot yours too."

"Ray, enchante again! Want to go for dinner?"

"Sounds like a plan."

"So, were you dumped by your travel-buddy?" he said with a wink.

"Well, we had just met in Hanoi and travelled to Sapa and Halong Bay together, so not really travel-buddies. That's the backpacking life no; you travel a bit together and then go your separate ways. Were you dumped by your buddy?"

"Well no, sort of the same story as you with the exception being not visiting Sapa."

"It's very nice, we trekked a lot."

"Ah, am not the trekking type."

"So, you're from India? Don't come across a lot of Indian backpackers."

"I am a Bengali, we are known in India for our wanderlust; though I must admit there's not an avid backpacking community yet in India."

"India is high on my list to visit! So, how is it to backpack there?"

"Umm, I actually wouldn't know, I've never backpacked yet in India."

"Actually I've never backpacked in Hungary either. I guess I like to travel someplace else."

"Oh, I have travelled a lot with my family in India while growing up. It's lovely!"

Maria was quite good company, interesting and smart; there was a good camaraderie between the two and the absence of a romantic spark kept things easy. Ray suggested his favourite restaurant facing the water and they continued their conversation there.

"Have a girlfriend back home in India?"

"I live in the Netherlands and no, have been single for a couple of years. What about you?"

"No boy back home either. You seem like a nice guy, how come?"

"Hmm, I've got that question quite often the past few days! I think though I can attract women for the initial relation, it's tough to find someone to stay with."

"Are you difficult?"

"Umm, I think I am easy to get along with, but one gets comfortable in their ways after being single and living alone for a while."

"So no commitment issues?" she said with a smile.

"I think not, I mean I begin relations with the intention of something longer, but it doesn't work out. I am getting a bit date-tired."

"Oh, I know the feeling. I think it's difficult to meet someone who you really like and who is at the same stage as you."

"How true!"

Ray was a bit relieved that he was not the only one at odds with the relation and settling thing.

Their food came; today Ray had ordered fresh spring-rolls, which consisted of charcoaled meat and chicken together with vegetables enwrapped in sticky rice-paper.

"I love Hoi An," he said while devouring a mouthful.

"Me too, only I've been shopping like crazy."

"Me too, only now I am thinking how to carry it."

"Just ship it back, like I am doing."

"Well, someone is taking care of my apartment, so I guess she could receive the package when it arrives."

"It's so cheap and good here; I love the silk dresses. By the way, don't ship wooden things, as they might not be allowed to ship due to termites."

"Umm, I've only got cloth so far. Though perhaps I'll buy one of the cool lanterns but that has some wood, but I could carry it in my back-pack," he said sounding out his thoughts.

After eating, the pair went on a shopping spree; Ray bought a lantern and a silk dressing gown. They then passed by the tailor shop where Ray had given the order. The funny shop-girl was there and started flirting, "Hand-sum man, you come to try fitting?"

"Yes," said Ray with a blush.

The first suit had been made as also one of the shirts. Ray tried on a light blue shirt with the navy blue suit. It was exactly the tapering look and finish as they had selected on the catalogue. Ray was so happy that he wanted to get some extra shirts and suits made. He chose a linen material for the suit, of a light blue colour and three more silk based shirts, bringing his grand total to three suits and eight shirts. He calculated that it would still cost him less than a single branded suit back home.

"I want to ship it."

"No problem, you come back tomorrow, we call courier service."

"Will everything be ready by then?"

"Of course."

Ray again felt a pang of remorse, for these people worked everyday for long hours, smiling all the time for a fraction of a salary in Europe. He considered how life was unfair, the place where you were born determined the amount of comfort you would have in your life. However, the sobering thought was that these people were happy and had the motivation to go further in life and succeed.

He did not negotiate at all this time and just accepted the price they quoted.

Leaving the shop, Ray walked Maria to her hostel, which was nearby. They arranged to meet again the next day, to further see the sights, go to the local market and generally hang out.

"G'night."

"G'night."

Chuc mung nam moi

The next morning Maria and Ray started early in the morning at the local market, which was an organised chaos of chicken sellers, vegetables farmers, artwork, spices, dried animal parts and the ubiquitous noodle-soup eatery. Maria absolutely loved the ambience. The market was geared towards local clientele and the two squeezed their way through the crowds. They came across a vendor selling handicrafts and Ray decided to buy some table-mats, beautifully hand-embroidered on silk.

"I anyway will ship the clothes tonight and I'll send these also along," he said, justifying his retail therapy to Maria.

Maria proceeded to buy an assortment of items and said, "For my friends and I'm shipping tonight too," she said with a laugh.

Hoi An and the next couple of days passed cheerfully. The pair cycled around town, to the beach, got an odd massage, gorged on the lovely local palate and basically relaxed.

"Shall we move on to the next place?" asked Maria one fine morning.

"I was thinking the same. I was planning to head to Nga Trang, it's a beach town."

"Yeah, I've heard of that. Umm, I was planning to go more into the countryside through the mountains around Dalat and perhaps take an easy riders tour."

"What's that?"

"Not that, but who, they are local guides who travel on motorcycles and take you to small villages on the back on their motorcycles."

"So you sit with your backpack mounted on a motorcycle as they make their way around mountains?"

"Yes, you sound sceptical. Where's your sense of adventure?" said Maria with a wink.

"Well for me the whole sabbatical experience is an adventure. I guess, I don't like taking unnecessary risks . . . For instance I don't want to do bungy jumping, though of course this isn't like that. I don't know, I was looking forward to the beach, I had a great time in Thailand's beaches."

"Well, of course you should do what you want to do"

"Are you planning to go to Saigon after that?"

"I don't know, I might cross over to Cambodia. I am not that much into big cities."

"Well, perhaps we meet in Cambodia again then. I plan to get there too."

"Sure."

They had a big hug goodbye; Ray quite liked the easy-going and adventurous spirit of Maria. They parted and Ray went back to the hotel where they were putting up decorations for the New Year which was in a couple of days.

"I am going to check out, as I am leaving tomorrow morning."

"You don't stay for New year?" said the pretty receptionist and made a pout to make her case

He smiled and said, "Next time. I am off to Nga Trang."

"Oh, it will be very busy there."

"Probably expensive prices at hotels then . . . Say, how do you say Happy New Year in Vietnamese?"

"Chuc mung nam moi."

"Chuc mung nam moi?" Ray repeated slowly.

"Very good! Shall I book your bus seat for tonight?"

"Yes please."

Ray packed his belongings into the backpack again and though he had shipped off the new-made clothes, it was as heavy as before due to the sundry things he had bought in Hoi An. He was all set to hit the beach in Nga Trang, further in sunny South Vietnam.

Separating him from that that was a long journey in a night bus . . . the travails of travelling!

Ray mentally prepared himself for a rickety ride as he made his way to the bus-station. A group of travellers was gathered there; such rides also made for great stories and camaraderie between the travellers. Ray wanted to again take an upper berth, as taking the lower deck on his previous night-bus trip had seen him surrounded by ticketless squatters.

He quickly discovered that this bus had a large upper deck in the back, which could probably accommodate four to five persons side by side. However, he wanted some privacy, so decided to take a window upper seat which was located just before this deck. The deck got filled with a young Swiss couple and another French one further away from Ray. The Swiss girl was quite effervescent and got chatting to all her neighbours immediately as the usual introduction round was done. Her name was Saskia and she said that she was visiting her boyfriend who was doing an internship in Vietnam. Her boyfriend was snoring happily, obviously quite experienced in night-bus rides. Ray could not sleep much either, so he passed most of the ride chatting with Saskia.

Eventually they got some sleep and early in the next morning they were dropped off at the hotel area. Ray could smell the nearby sea and though early morning, he could sense the warmth and humidity of this beach town.

The staff of the hotel where they had been dropped off tried to get as many passengers for their rooms, but most of the passengers hastily left for hostels. "We take care of you," said the receiving staff guy from the hotel to Ray.

Ray decided to take a look, the room was on the second floor, was small and they were charging a hefty premium due to the upcoming New Year, but it was clean and Ray was too tired to go hotel-searching, so he made a deal with air-conditioning thrown in.

As he had not slept much, he decided to get a beauty sleep, opting for the beach rather than in the room. As he made his way downwards from the room, he met the Swiss couple, who had also taken a room in the same hotel and also had the idea to go to the beach for a slumber.

They passed a facial parlour on the same road as the hotel. Ray figured that beach-towns would be his beauty places, earlier Phuket in Thailand and now here. He was also getting very tanned, turning a shade of brown to which his Dutch neighbour normally said, "Zo ordinair hoor"[20] when Ray would return from a warm and sunny vacation.

They arrived at the beach as the Sun was beginning to come out and glow brightly. It was an immense beach with fine, white sand though the water was a bit rough, a bit of a contrast to the calm emerald green in Thailand. There were not too many people as yet as it was still early morning. They stretched out their sarangs and dozed off to the sound of the water splashing against the beach.

Ray awoke to the chatter of Dutch sounds and he sat up with curiosity, only to see the two Dutch girls he had met on one of the night-buses. His heart started racing a bit faster at the sight of the smaller one whom he fancied; she wore a polka-dot bikini and had become more tanned and her hair more blond than he recollected in the night he had first seen her.

"He hoi!" he exclaimed.

The two girls jumped a bit, possibly at the sudden Dutch greeting from a brown man and gradually a look of recognition seemed to dawn.

"Why hello! The Dutch-Indian guy from the bus from Hanoi to Hue," said the tall one.

"Wow, good memory!"

Saskia, who like Ray had not slept much on the bus, also got up while her boyfriend Sigfried who had slept almost the entire journey continued his solid sleep.

"Hi I am Saskia," she introduced herself, always the jovial one.

"Floor," said the tall one.

"Eefke," said the pretty one.

---

[20] Literally meaning "So ordinary," but said with a tongue in cheek to the North European tourists who go to the beaches and get very tanned

"Ray."

Sigfried snorted in agreement and turned in his sleep.

"Saskia is a Dutch name," said Floor.

"Also Swiss."

The usual pleasantries and backpacker questions ensued. Ray found it hard to gaze away from Eefke.

"Actually it's our last day here today; we're off to Mui Ne with the night bus tonight," she said.

"Oh but I just arrived here . . ."

"You took a long time en route."

After some more small-talk, the Dutch girls went on jogging further on the beach.

"Hmmmm," sighed Ray.

"You liked the small one?"

"Yeah."

"The tall one was eyeing you."

"Really? I didn't notice . . ."

"She was!"

"Story of my life; the girls I like are not interested in me and vice-versa."

"Sounds awful! By the way, we were thinking of doing a boat-tour of the surrounding islands tomorrow, want to join?" she said helpfully, trying to change the topic.

"Sure, it's a great way to go Island hopping!"

"I've heard that Mui Ne is quite nice too, also with the New Year's celebrations."

"That's in a couple of days already right? I think I'll stick around here till then; I like getting the feel of places."

"Don't you want to follow the small blond?" she said with a wink.

Ray smiled and said, "Well, perhaps we'll meet again if it's destined. So, let's grab breakfast and book an Island tour for tomorrow or so."

"Need to wake up sleepy-head first; it's freaking not fair that he sleeps so well!" said Saskia looking at the sleeping Sigfried.

They found a 24-hour Pho (Noodle soup) restaurant, quite modern and on the same street as their hotel to the beach.

"Food is so cheap here compared to Switzerland," observed Sigfried.

"Food is cheap everywhere compared to Switzerland," said Ray who had recently been to Zurich on a short-trip.

They parted and thereafter Ray had a relaxing day, and went to get a facial where as usual the beautician called him "hand-sum." He wondered if they meant it or were doing it just for the tips.

The Island tour the next day was similar to the one in Phuket, a day full of adjoining Islands and beaches, one prettier than the other. This one included a trip to a sort of sea world. It was designed in the shape of a Pirate ship and inside were fish and creatures of sea in tanks of all sizes. As he passed through the tanks, he suddenly froze as a small shark loomed past. While there was hard glass separating them, they was something sinister about this fish, especially accentuated by the film Jaws which made Ray shiver a bit.

Menacing shark in tank

There was also an outdoor pool/aquarium of sorts, infested by sharks and like, with more swimming freedom than the tanks inside. Ray noticed a shark, resting on top of a enormous sea-turtle. They seemed to be in harmony; perhaps these sinister looking fish were misunderstood after all, he thought.

Back on the boat, there was a sumptuous lunch of a multitude of sea-food and fruit and thereafter came the big surprise and most evident difference to the Thai tour. The food was cleared and the boat deck was converted into an impromptu stage and the guide started singing. It was Asian karaoke at its best, as he belted out Titanic's "My heart will go on" and songs to the like.

Then, if that was not cheesy enough, they opened a drinking session in the water. All the tourists were encouraged to join into the sea, where they were given shots of cheap rice-Vodka. Saskia and Sigfried joined the revelries; Ray just sat in the Sun and enjoyed the cool sea-breeze. For the last stop, all the touring boats converged on an Island, replete with white sand, beach-chairs, cocktails shacks and a volleyball arena. Saskia, effervescent as ever, started collecting a group of people, also from other boats to engage in a game. Ray, still full from the lunch, reluctantly agreed. In his team, he recognized an Australian couple he had met earlier in Phuket, Thailand.

"Howdy mate, we meet again!"

"Small world eh?"

"Yeah, we've been beach-crawling, from Phuket, we went to the East coast to Ko Samui and Ko Phangan and then to Cambodia and then here in Vietnam."

Ray's thoughts floated to Daphne, he wondered where she was; last heard she had gone to Ko Samui.

Switching back to the conversation, he asked, "Australia has some lovely beaches too, how come you travel to S.E. Asia and not go to the local beaches?"

"Mate, it's so expensive back home. We live in Perth, the flights to here are almost as expensive as flying across the country and once here, it's so cheap."

"Ah, that's why I've come across so many Aussi's here."

"Bali's a big favourite amongst us"

"Right, I plan to go there perhaps too."

They played some volleyball only very briefly, as Saskia had the impulse to kick the ball when she could not reach a spike with her hands and the ball took an alternative trajectory and disappeared into the trees. The players went looking into the trees, which were infested with loads of mosquitoes and the search party came back covered in red-bulges all over. It was good entertainment all in all though and in the evening they all had dinner together at one of the restaurants in town.

The next morning, when Ray woke up late and sauntered down to the hotel reception area, one of the guys from the hotel asked him if he would like a tour of the area.

"With bike?"

"Yes."

"Ok, let's do it. I am Ray, what's your name?"

"Hung."

The tour took them across a bridge to the north part of town, which had the Po Nagar Cham towers, a place used for Hindu worship. There was a very impressive view of the bridges and water with the mountains in the backdrop.

View from bridge in Nha Trang

The guys took some shots posing as crazy tourists against the backdrop of the ancient towers. It was a warm and lovely day. Afterwards they made their way to the Long Son Pagoda, which was a brilliant wooden structure decorated with elegant designs in collared glass. Behind the pagoda there was a hill, on top of which there was a Giant Buddha. Ray climbed up the hill alongside other local pilgrims and paid his homage to the big white Buddha. Two very children were playing along Ray and he took a photo of them,

Giant Buddha statue with children playing in front

After these sights, Ray was taken back to the hotel.
"So, are you working full-time at the hotel?" asked Ray of Hung.

"No, I study, and sometimes work. Now, its holidays because of New Year. What work you do?"

"I work in a sales role back home."

"I think you important man, make lot of money."

Ray smiled.

Hung smiled and emphasized, "I think you make more than thousand dollars per month."

"Umm, slightly more," Ray was embarrassed that there is such a big discrepancy at salaries around the world. People worked so hard here in Vietnam, all days of the week with a big smile. They had holidays once a year during the New Year which they spent getting back home, re-painting and repairing their houses. He most decidedly had a cushy life in Utrecht, he reflected.

He then continued on the beach for the afternoon, dozing mostly. Ray chose a spot under a coconut tree, a bit further up the beach, while the Swiss couple lay a bit further in full glory of the Sun. After awhile he sat up to stretch a bit and there was a girl looming in front of him.

She asked, "Do you have a fire?"

"Ja hoor,"[21] he replied with a wink.

"Oh, how did you know I was Dutch?"

"Your dun-glish gave you away. There seem to be a lot of Dutchies here."

"Well, Sun, sand and sex eh! The three 's' vacation as we say." She waved to her friend, who joined her. "You'll like her, she's Asian too and very hot."

The Asian friend was petite and looked like a mix of Western and Asian descent. Ray thought, 'Mixed-breeds make for an exciting combination' when he glanced at her. She was petite and curvaceous and with her nose piercing and Lolita-like look was indeed hot as her friend suggested.

She had heard what her friend had said and spoke, "I don't like Asian men, they're small," and for extra elucidation, demonstrated what she meant by pointing her little finger upwards. "And they

---

[21]   Yes indeed

think I am a hooker, I have been asked quite often here how much I charge." Her name was Yoriko, she was Japanese and spoke English with an American accent.

This seemed to be the season for boisterous girls. The two girls made for an odd couple; the tall Dutch Maaike lanky and well-built, probably brought up on a protein rich staple diet of meat, potatoes and boiled vegetables while petite Yoriko probably brought up on a diet of raw-fish (sushi) and rice. In character though, Ray could not ascertain much variance. Boisterous, demonstrative and keen to speak their minds, they had met each other during a wild party in Laos and continued the good life since. They had picked up a gang of partying backpacker's en-route to Nga Trang; there was a German fella replete with a beard and a deep voice, a Finnish twin with unpronounceable names and a pale looking Brit couple. Coupled with tanned Ray and the Swiss Saskia and Sigfired, and under a coconut tree the gang looked like a scene from the Film 'The Beach', except the obvious fact that this was not a marooned island.

The gaiety and revelry continued for the next hours as tumblers were downed to wash down the sea-food. Ray eventually ventured to eat the fresh crab and lobster cooked directly on the beach and served with a spicy sauce, the taste was so sumptuous that he closed his eyes to enjoy the feeling. One of the Finnish twins had the brilliant idea to create a fruit cocktail, quite literally cutting the local fruit in half and after scooping a bit of the fruit-pulp, replacing that portion with rice-vodka and thereafter eating/drinking the entirety.

That evening Ray gave away his T-shirts to an orphanage, he reckoned they would be put to good usage for the upcoming New Year. The face of the person accepting the clothes was so radiant that Ray had to hold back tears as he remembered the handicapped man from Hoi An.

The partying continued the next couple of days and then New Year's Eve came and if the solar version in Bangkok had been a bit of a simple affair, the lunar Vietnamese version broke all records of partying. Dragons, bands, dancing, fire-juggling and of course cocktails were in the line-up, culminating in a grand finale of spectacular fireworks on the beach at midnight. Nga Trang was one of the favourite spot for locals to experience New Year's too and the beach was full of revellers including the backpacking gang of Ray's.

At a wee hour in the morning when the crowds started to fade, Ray got himself a temporary tattoo. It was of an archer shooting from a chariot and it looked suspiciously like the Burberry logo. The party slowly came to an end and the group made their way back to their abodes. While the rest was lodging across the street from the beach in a hostel, Ray's hotel was a bit further away.

As he walked merrily and drunken onwards, he was suddenly conscious of a local girl approaching him and also noticed a group of men further away. Alarm bells started ringing, as he had heard of single men being hustled; the procedure being that of initially a girl getting coy and touchy and thereafter the hapless man being deprived of his belongings by either the soft pickpocket way or hard with the help of accomplices.

Ray did not fancy either and the panic had a sobering effect on him. He quickened his pace and glared menacingly at the approaching girl. It had the desired effect and the girl and her posse slowed down. Ray reached a well-lit square with lot of locals still around and he breathed a sigh of relief. A group of teenagers were playing around with a football. One of them looked at Ray curiously trying to place his looks.

"Chuc mung nam moi," ventured Ray.

"Chuc mung nam moi," said the boy, his eyes lighting up. "Wow, your Vietnamese is very good"

"Thanks, you speak good English. That's about the extent of my Vietnamese; I can also say Thank you, but nobody understands that."

"Cảm ơn?"

"Yes, though when I say it, it comes out as 'Come on'."

"Well, welcome to Vietnam."

"Thanks!"

The boy was the son of a family who had returned to live in Vietnam from the US. Ray wondered whether he would ever return to India.

"Mate, I am absolutely wasted," said Ray after a short chat. "Have fun!" he said as he bid the revellers goodbye.

"Have fun!"

He woke up in the morning with his head bonging like an Indian rubber ball. After a long, warm shower during which his cheap tattoo got completely erased, he made his way to the Pho (noodle soup) place, just the perfect cure for the hangover. He took a seat outside, the staff knew him by this time, and he ordered his usual soup and black coffee floating over sweet condensed milk. There was an older local couple also sitting outside. The man was quite chatty and asked Ray the usual where from, what you do questions.

"What about you? Your English is quite good," asked Ray.

"Well, I am originally from here, that is, I was born here, but my family migrated after the war to the US when I was two. Five decades later, I decided to come back and retire to the motherland."

"Ah," Ray wondered whether the youngster he had met the previous night was their offspring. "Was it difficult to adjust back, a reverse culture shock?"

"Oh my God yes! I only knew Vietnam from my family, for a long time we could not come back as my family is from South Vietnam. Then we used to come back for vacations once in a while, but that's very different from living here now."

"What are the differences?"

"Everything!"

"What do you particularly find difficult?"

"The red tape and slowness of things I think. It takes ages to get anything and if I complain about it, the officials, 'Go back to where you came from'." He paused for effect and then reiterated. "Go back to where you came from!"

Ray could not help but smile at the theatrics.

"It's the daily things which are difficult, commuting, water supply, electricity and oh, did I mention red-tape?"

"So, are you considering going back?"

"Ah no, I am quite happy here with the extended family, retired and my kids are going to school. Good weather and food and it's a better quality of life overall."

"Sounds good actually."

"So, you like Vietnam?"

"Well I got off to a cold start in the North but quite warming up now."

They parted and Ray made his way to the beach where sure enough, the boisterous girls and the gang were up engaging in the ritual of Sun God worship. This was going to be the last day for some as some were going to Mui Ne and some others to Saigon or Northwards.

"I think I'll take the night bus to Saigon tonight too," said Ray.

"Let's have a big farewell party," said Maaike.

The thing about the backpacking community is that you make friends for life only to part a couple of days later. They made their way to an Indian restaurant as the group was in the mood for a good curry. Ray happily agreed as after weeks of noodles, he was in the mood for a Roti. He ordered a Saag Murg, a perennial favourite of his from the Indian cuisine, chicken and spinach cooked in an assortment of typical Indian spices. He hoped that it would bear some resemblance to the original from India. The staff of Indian origin did not disappoint or perhaps it was due to the nice change from the staple diet of the past weeks but whatever the reason it was fabulous.

"Mmmm," said Yoriko to her meal.

"Mm mm," joined the chorus

Thereafter they went to their favourite bar in Nha Trang, which was appropriately called "Why not." Ray really liked the phrase, he was want of saying 'pourquoi pas or porque no'[22] depending on the audience. The owner greeted them like long-lost friends as they had been the biggest source of revenue over the past days.

"Chuc mung nam moi," said Ray.

---

[22] Why not in French and Spanish respectively

"Chuc mung nam moi my friends. For you happy hour all evening," which meant two drinks for the price of one.

Afterwards, well fed and tipsy, the posse made their way to the busses and though the acquaintance had been brief, it had been strong. They all hugged each other. Especially Maaike and Yoriko bid a tearful farewell, as the former was going to Mui Ne and the latter to Saigon.

It was back to basic style Vietnamese style sleeper bus as Ray gingerly put his foot inside the hole. All the upper berth seats were already occupied, so Ray mentally prepared himself to be surrounded by chicken and other produce. This time however, the bus did not get packed to the brim; probably the locals were still celebrating with their families he figured. Ray slept like a baby, perhaps it was the gentle rocking of the bus or perhaps it was the percentage alcohol in his system, in any case it worked.

Saigon and onto Cambodia

Ray awoke with a startle in middle of the night; the bus had stopped for a break. This bus had much more spacious seats, however on the downside there was no toilet on board. 'It was probably for the better, as it spared the stinking feeling,' thought Ray.

Realising his chance to unload, he took off with a start, exclaimed 'pi-pi' to the driver and escaped to the nearest field. There were cows mooing in the distance and the stars were shining in the clear dark sky. Ray was appreciating this peaceful world view when suddenly there was a rustle in the bushes in front. Ray jumped back with a start, fearing he had interrupted the sleep of some noble countryside animal; only to see a fellow traveller of the fairer species emerging from the twig, apparently having had the same inspiration as Ray.

"No toilet on bus," she said stating the obvious.

Ray shrugged his shoulder in accordance to this apposition of the situation.

"Let's get back before he takes off without us."

They whisked through the mud and re-boarded the waiting bus. Ray promptly went back to his drunken monk deep sleep. He even woke himself up due to his own snoring. It was probably even worse for his fellow travellers and the ticketless locals squatting on the floor. 'Sweet revenge for the previous times that they kept me awake with their chatter,' he thought and smiled, as he meandered back to sleep again.

The next time he awoke, they had apparently reached Saigon. Ray alighted from the bus half-asleep, half-awake. What a name

Saigon, conjured up a thousand images, also made popular by the musical Ms. Saigon. It was called Ho Chi Minh City now, but most locals seemed to call it Saigon still. Ray preferred the old name too; as he never had warmed to the idea of places, airports, etc. being named after persons.

Tet, (the Vietnamese New Year) celebrations were still on for the entire week, so prices were still hiked up as he found out with the hostels and hotels he engaged in conversations with. In the end, he found one with a room without any windows but with air-conditioning for a decent price and dropped off his stuff there. After the mandatory morning three-S's (shitting, showering and shaving), he went out for breakfast.

"Aye Ray!" said this very familiar voice from behind. It was Yann!

"Aye aye!"

The buddies hugged each other like long lost friends.

"Where's your French love?" asked Ray looking over Yann's shoulder.

"Ah you know, vacation romance, finito now and she's gone back home."

"So, you're a free bird again."

"I was always a free bird! Where's the Hungarian?"

"Probably in Cambodia by now."

"Did you . . . ?" inquired Yann, his voice trailing away in expectation of a juicy story.

"Nah, she was a good friend, plus I told you, I was taking a break from vacation romances." He paused and said pensively, "You know, this sabbatical is not a vacation, but a lifestyle."

"You mean, live like a bum?" Yann said with a wink.

"You've got to get these Pulp Fiction quotes out of your head!"

Yann laughed and continued, ". . . but tell me, why is this not a vacation?"

"Well, the thing is, a vacation is about sight-seeing or relaxing or adventure sports . . ."

". . . and this is not . . . ?"

"Well, it is, but different."

"Same same, but different! You sound like the shop-keepers here."

"Umm, I am trying to form my thoughts. You see, it's about getting to a new place without a major plan, eating, drinking, sleeping, travelling etc without the comforts of home or of vacations. With a vacation, it is a short, finite period after which you are going back to daily life."

"So the difference is the duration?"

"Amongst other things; for a two or three weeks vacations, you are 'escaping daily life' for that period, but somehow you have it at the back or your head. With this version, it's somewhere a blob on the horizon."

"I see your point. What else?"

"Umm, the lifestyle . . . Every place I go to I decide there and then to stay as long as it's nice. That has implications for planning and also for engaging with others, locals and other travellers"

"So you want to continue this lifestyle?" asked Yann earnestly.

"I would like to, but I don't have sufficient money to retire," Ray said wryly.

"Well, maybe you should write a book about your travel? You express yourself well; I have been following your travel blog."

"Thanks, though writing a book is a different cup of tea. Plus, secondly there are so many travel books, why would anyone buy mine if there's a Lonely Planet around?"

"You should make it an adventure book, not a travel book."

"Hmmm," Ray's mind was ticking. "Perhaps I should."

"And then you can become a millionaire and live the bum lifestyle."

"Well, I don't know if I'll like this period to be forever but the idea of not having to work anymore for a living is tempting."

"I can't say I know you through and through, but I think you are someone who needs it all; both challenging work and hobbies at the same time."

"You are probably right. So, I will embark on this new hobby!"

"And I will say later to my friends that I know a famous author. You must feature me in your book."

"I will mon ami, I will. In India we have an expression, sometimes people you met yesterday are friends for life."

"I am honoured," said Yann with a small bow, "and you can add all your romantic conquests."

Ray could not help but smile. He reflected, "Mostly a case of missed chances. Come, let's grab some breakfast, I am starved!"

"I know just the place for great Pho."

"Not pho again!"

"They also have spring rolls."

"Let's go then. When did you come here?"

"Yesterday evening; I was planning to see the sights today."

"Great, I had a decent sleep on the bus, so let's do that after breakfast."

The boys had a good fresh breakfast and thereafter went to see the "Notre Dame," a church built by the French, as the name suggested. A couple of years back the statue was reported to have shed tears which are created a big commotion and traffic chaos. There was no such luck on this day so the boys just posed before the lady.

Notre Dame in Saigon

Nearby was the Post-office, a well-maintained colonial style building and then they made their way through Le Loi, which is the main street-name in all cities in Vietnam and sat down on a bench to soak in the ambience. This was the picture of Asia on the rise, modern skyscrapers looming in the distance against the multitude of people celebrating the New Year festivities.

Bustling Saigon

"You like it?" inquired Yann.

"Umm, I had a different image of Saigon, the name conjures up images of a quaint old place, but this is a modern bustling metropolis."

"I have the same feeling. But my holidays are almost coming to an end, so let's party one more time!"

"When are you leaving?"

"In two days."

"Ok, then I'll stay two days too and then head to Cambodia."

"I envy you! So, will you take the bus to Cambodia?"

"Actually I was thinking of going by boat, taking a two to three day tour of the Mekong River starting in Vietnam and culminating in Phnom Phen."

"Wow! This bum life sounds quite good."

In the evening, the boys went for dinner and then to the party area of downturn. There were American style huge bars blaring loud music, much to their distaste. Suddenly Ray saw the Dutch girls he had met on the bus to Hue and thereafter in Nga Trang briefly, the tall and the shorter one. They were sitting at a bar with another girl and a tall bloke.

He indicated them to Yann and whispered, "Let's divide and conquer, I quite like the smaller of the two, so why don't you go for the taller one?"

"Sure, I anyways always end up with a blond girl."

"Umm, they're both blond, though the third one is a brunette."

"Oui oui, make your move."

The boys made their way to the table and Ray exclaimed, "Small world eh, we meet again!"

"Hey!"

"Hey!"

Ray sat down next to Eefke, the smaller one, while Yann next to Floor. The brunette, Ellen was a bubbly girl who had met the other girls in Saigon. The bloke was from Australia and seemed friendly, though perhaps a bit perturbed at suddenly having to compete for the attention of the girls.

The music was loud and everybody had to sort of shout to make themselves audible to their conversation partners. Floor and Ellen were engaging with Ray while Eefke was asking Yann about his travels. After a brief while, she suggested exchanging seats and Ray obliged, thinking it to be temporary. He took the seat between Floor and Ellen while Eefke was now seated between Yann and the Aussi bloke. They were both competing for her attention and she was basking in the glory.

Ray was getting his own attention from the other two girls; and he thought of the theory of games from Malcolm Nash, made popular by the film 'A beautiful mind.'

Yann looked at Ray for acknowledgement and Ray nodded, realizing that Eefke's attention was solely focused on the blokes around her. Now that he was out of the game with Eefke, Ray at least wanted Yann to win over the Aussi bloke. Cocktails kept coming and Ray was feeling the effects of the bus-ride.

"I think I am going to head back to the hotel," he said eventually, resigned to his loss.

"I'll walk with you," said Floor. Ray saw a glimmer of hope for the evening still ending with a score.

"I think I'll join you too," said Ellen, who was staying in the same hotel as the girls. Ray's glimmer of hope evaporated with the speed of camphor when exposed to air.

"I think I'll stay a bit longer," said Eefke. Yann and the Aussi bloke wholeheartedly agreed to keep her company.

"Well, ciao then."

"Ciao." "Ciao." "Ciao." "Ciao."

Ray walked the girls to their hotel and went back to his and contemplated what it could have been. His thoughts wandered to Hilary and especially to Daphne who, last heard before Facebook was blocked in Vietnam, was undergoing a health treatment on the Thai islands. He wondered whether he would ever meet that special someone for the longer term or whether he was destined to stay alone. Not that he had a bad life, far from it, he loved the variety and did not mind being alone, but it was in moments like this that he felt lonely.

The next morning he slept in and went for breakfast at the place where Yann had taken him the previous day. Sure enough, there was Yann there, waiting for Ray.

"I am sorry mate; we French are not good wing-men."

"You treacherous bastard," said Ray not too seriously. "So, who won the battle?"

"Well, as I told you, I always end up with the blond girl," Yann grinned ear to ear.

"Good for you."

"I am leaving tomorrow, I want to part as friends."

"But of course, don't worry, it was a bit disappointing, but hey that's life."

"C'est la vie quoi."[23]

"So we have one evening before you leave; do you have plans with Eefke?"

"No no, no plans, why don't we have a good dinner. I can't party as I have an early flight."

---

[23]   French for "That's life"

"I also booked a Mekong Delta tour, the trouble with tours is that they are fully-packed; so it's also leaving early at dawn."

"Why did you book a tour then and not travel on your own like you do?"

"I am getting lazy," said Ray with a wink. "No actually, I just thought it would be easier to cross the border with an organized agency."

The amigos spent the day relaxing and chatting and talking about Ray's book, Yann was full of ideas to spice it up.

"Why don't you write one yourself?" asked Ray.

"Ah no, I think you are great story-teller. I am a technical guy."

"Well, so am I originally."

For dinner they went to a place where the main novelty was grilling marinated fish; it was just like how they had started in Hanoi. Over the grill and local beer, Ray said, "I am not good at goodbyes, so I'll say it now, I really enjoyed meeting you."

"The same here! Come to Paris soon."

"And you to the Netherlands."

"Let's raise a glass to Vietnam!"

"And to travelling!"

The boys parted.

The next morning, Ray woke at dawn and was picked up to be taken to the Mekong tour. As he sat in the back of the bus in a state of semi asleep; he thought about how this country had grown on him after the initial cold shock up North. Another chapter of his travels was closing and once again he had mixed feeling, while he was a bit sad to leave, he also looked forward to getting to Cambodia, especially to the temples of Angor.

The Mekong delta was the rice-bowl of Vietnam, in fact if their guide was to be believed, a bad production here would affect the world supply of rice. They passed small towns with lush fields of paddy. Rivers were the cradles of civilizations in ancient times before the advents of road, rail or air and one could see the usage of the Mekong and its various tributaries still in the same vein. Small boats were the mode of transport, there were floating markets, even floating villages and humans and cows washed in the river.

Boats on the Mekong river

Paddy needs to sub merged in water in order to grow and this humid and rain-aplenty region was perfect for it. It also made for annoying mosquitoes as Ray hastily put repellent deet cream and took his first Malarone pill. He had just enough pill supply to last through Cambodia which was the only country in his travel so far to carry a Malaria warning.

After the boat ride of floating villages and markets, they went ashore to a candy making factory which was also selling various liquors with assorted arthropods fermenting inside the bottles.

Assorted liquors with arthropods

If that was not enough to evoke the queasy feeling, the next stop was at a crocodile farm. It was literally a farm, that is, crocodiles were harvested for their meat and leather. When approaching the enclosures, there was already a stench of the reptiles but the sight when they reached the cages was horrifying. There were swarms of crocodiles wading in the enclosures half filled with water and everywhere they were bird chicks which were their feed. The crocodiles would just kill those little chicks, some they ate, and other chicks were just floating dead. 'So much for the fallacy that animals just kill when they are hungry,' thought Ray. 'In the end humans were probably the worst offenders, but the image was simply horrifying.'

Crocodile farm

They stopped for the night in a small town, almost on the border with Cambodia. There was a bunch of Spanish people in the group, unmistakable due to their audibility. Ray joined them as he wanted to practice a bit of Spanish. They went searching for a restaurant however all of them were closed due to the New Year celebrations still. Nobody spoke a word of English and the guide was fast asleep in his room, tired from having had to wake up the earliest.

Eventually, through sign-language they found a place to eat and were treated to possibly the best meal in Vietnam. It was a festivity of fresh fish with authentic spices and rice. People is small towns were much friendlier than the ones in bigger cities and here was no exception. The bill was in the end also extremely light on the pockets even for Vietnamese standards and the party sauntered well-fed and content to their quarters. Ray had an electronic repellent with him whom he had originally bought from India and he lighted it and slept like a well-fed Cheshire cat.

The next morning they were taken to a Fish farm, which was not spectacular, but was good for some delirious splashing when the fish were fed. It was then time to transfer to the 'fast boat' for part of the group to go onto Cambodia. The rest were going by the cheaper bus option which would take longer. Besides the faster part, Ray thought it would be novel to cross a border by boat, his first time doing so. After an hour or so on the boat, they stopped at the border and off-boarded in order to get the Visa on arrival. It cost them two dollar more than it should have and for those without a photo, five dollars more. A tiny brush with corruption on this entire trip so far, however it beat hands-on the hassles of going to a consulate to sort out visas.

They boarded back to the boat and continued on the Mekong, now in the Cambodian part. There was no perceptible difference in the landscape, the boats, floating villages and huts that lined the river.

The Cambodian countryside as viewed from boat

Ray wondered whether the people would resemble more the Thai or the Vietnamese looks. The Cambodian guide cum tout who had boarded the boat at the border seemed somewhat darker than the average Vietnamese and had slightly more rounded features.

The 'fast boat' took eight hours in total to reach Phnom Penh; finally they arrived in the late afternoon. Four of the boat party including Ray had arranged with the tout to see some hotels and there was a mini-van waiting for them when they arrived.

Ray was tired after the long journey and waking up at five a.m. so wanted a room fast, with his only requirement being that it would be clean. A quick check-in was however not on the cards as the mini-bus taxi guy took the group from one place to another and all were full, it being high season, the tout explained. He then proceeded to take the mini-van on a touristic route, to drop off some gifts and Ray was getting increasingly frustrated. On the bright side, they were getting a tour of the city, the first impression being the golden roofed pagodas in the city, impressive boulevards and a huge palace ground in the city.

Ray was getting increasingly impatient and asked the driver to call up the next place beforehand before driving there to find out whether they had a room and somehow that tactic worked, there was a room. It was already getting dark and the room was clean with an attached bathroom and seemed cheap for the location and spaciousness. It was close to the palace grounds and other sights they had just passed, so Ray took the room.

Room in Phnom Phen

After showering and cleaning up, he went out to eat as he was famished. He walked towards the palace ground and found a clean-looking restaurant serving chicken dishes. He tucked in the sumptuous chicken dish served; it was a mix of the curry style of the Thai, but with a stir-fry element reminiscent of the light Vietnamese style.

When returning to the hotel, he got the inkling why the place was relatively cheap considering its location. The road was lined with massage places replete with bright red lights.

"You want boom-boom?" inquired one tout after another, being a different level of subtle than the previously heard, "Want happy ending?"

'Shoot, I've got myself a place a room on boom-boom boulevard,' he muttered to himself. The hotel itself seemed to bear some semblance of respectability, and besides Ray was dead-beat, so he decided to just stay and take it up with the hotel staff in the morning. He made doubly sure that the door was securely bolted and went off to sleep.

A country of contrast

It was a bright sunny day when he woke up in his spacious room. It was quite a new hotel, everything was quite clean. Ray got dressed and made his way to the reception area. Outside the hotel building, it seemed much more normal without the red-lights of the previous evening. He asked the receptionist that he wanted a normal massage without the happy ending or boom-boom to which she started laughing hysterically.

She summoned a masseur from a neighbouring provider and provided some instructions. The masseur beckoned to Ray to follow here, which he did tepidly. The parlour seemed quite innocent in broad daylight. Perhaps he had been imagining things the previous evening, he thought. He selected the Kymer massage which was six dollars.

The Khmer massage resembled more the arduous Thai one than the more relaxing Vietnamese one; Ray suspected that this was another of the things the Thais had copied when they sacked Angkor. Afterwards when he went to pay, he put in a dollar extra as tip; however the owner wanted more money. He pointed out on the price-list that the Kymer cost only six dollars and the owner looked at him confused. By the time, the masseur had come down and there was a brief exchange of information between the two and then the owner bowed and took the money with a smile.

It dawned on Ray that he was probably one of the very few customers who just took a normal massage; while the boom-boom variant probably being unlisted and higher in price. He wondered who would want a happy ending at this hour of the day, then realized that it was probably a destination for decadent westerners.

His heart went out for the poor women who performed the service. The world was just not fair.

His back sorted out, Ray exited the place and started walking further. He was suddenly confronted with old, decaying building covered in filth and squalor. It made such a contrast to the spic-and-span hotel he was lodging in.

He then went on a cult-tour and the temples were so grand and majestic. It was back to tuk-tuk time, though these tuk-tuks were a bit different from the Thai ones. While the Thai variant were tuk-tuks on one single integrated unit, the Cambodian ones had a motorcycle body housing the driver and fitted to a separate carriage for the passenger.

Once again Ray had such a deja-vu of Thailand while admiring the temples from afar. The sacking of Angkor was still a thorny issue between the modern nations, as the Thais made of with the artisans and craftsmen after the plundering, which was to shape Thai culture later.

Thereafter Ray went to the National Museum and it was brilliant, presenting a history of the nation, especially of Angkor. So far the Indianised Kingdoms of Thailand and Vietnam had been more leaning on Buddhism, whereas here the Angkor had a lot of Hindu deities like Vishnu, Shiva and the rest of the Indian Gods. The kings of Angkor proclaimed themselves to be Deva-Raja[24]. The name Angkor was derived from Nagara, meaning city in Sanskrit. At its peak, the temple cities of Angor had about a million people residing there, at a time when London counted a paltry fifty thousand. Ray quite looked forward to getting to Angkor or more accurately the town of Siem Reap, which was the base from which travellers took the tours of the Angkor temples.

It made such a contrast to the unfortunate history of Phnom Phen when it was ravished by the Khmer Rouge, made immortal by the film "The killing fields." It was weird to constantly experience such extreme contrasting feelings in a space of a day. It was getting quite hot in the afternoon, so Ray went to an Internet café to do some serious surfing, now that he was in a not-restricted Internet territory.

He eagerly opened Facebook and there was a note from Daphne from ages back and from Hilary more recently amongst a multitude of other posts. Hilary informed him that she had met someone else recently and it seemed to be working well and that she was sorry as Ray was such a nice guy. Ray had not expected a long-distance relation to work anyway even if he were home in the Netherlands, however coming on the heels of the debacle in Saigon; it still hit him as Hilary was such a lovely girl. 'Another one bites the dust,' he thought wryly.

The message from Daphne was somewhat vague, she was enjoying the good life on Ko Samui Island on the Thai East coast at the time of writing, and the tourists there had become a bit marooned due to the high-waves occurring as a result of the monsoons. She was planning to hit the road again once normal boat services resumed. He wrote to her explaining his whereabouts and said that he hoped to see her again, perhaps in Siem Riep.

He had kept in contact with his parents and sister while in Vietnam through sms-text, now wrote them an updated update on his travails. He then caught up on the rest of the correspondence

---

[24] Translated to God-King in Sanskrit

and wrote a blog entry. His blog had been viewed in a few thousands now and it just increased his desire to write a book. There was also a message from Maria, the Hungarian girl. She was presently also in Cambodia, at the beach town of Sihanoukvile. She was quite enthusiastic about it in the mail and asked Ray to join her. He wrote back saying he would in a couple of days.

After the hottest hours had passed, he made his way to the harbour, where children were playing on the square against the backdrop of the Mekong, while tourists and grown-up locals sauntered about.

Skyline of Phnom Phen

From there he made his way to the local markets, which were as usual in Asia a hub of activities, vendors plying their fruits and vegetables while motorcycles zipped past the hapless tourists and locals alike. It was less crowded then the counterparts in Vietnam and smelled less of fish than the ones in Thailand. Next to the markets were restaurants with touts beckoning to the lure of Angkor beer. Everything of pride in this country seemed to be called Angkor.

Ray went into one of the restaurants which seemed to house a lot of locals too and ordered a meal for the grand price of two dollars. Dollar was the going currency in Cambodia and it was nice not to have to mentally convert thousands of dongs as in Vietnam. A cocktail with fresh fruit cost another dollar and Ray was quite content with the food quality versus price. Food was the cheapest in Cambodia from the three countries he had visited so far. His food arrived, he had ordered a chicken dish and it was served with aromatic Khmer spices and in gravy of fresh coconut milk. The scent of lemon grass was unmistakable, the other flavours being more like the Thai ones. Ray again wondered in the line of his first thoughts which cuisine came first and had influenced the other.

Having had a heavy dinner he decided to leg it back to his hotel though it was quite a substantial way away. Phnom Phen was luckily not as big as Bangkok, after passing the walls of the palace he reached a big square which was full of groups of people exercising to music under the guidance of a leader. Phnom Phen was such a city of contrasts! Ray sat down, a bit weary from his long walk in the humid weather. The nearby fountains were lighted in red and green, alternating in brilliant cadence. Afterwards he made his way back to 'boom-boom' boulevard where he was accosted by the calls of massage. He smiled and walked to his hotel. Soon his hotel room was resonating to the sound of his gentle snoring, the effect of a long walking day coupled with a heavy meal.

✦

The next day was bright and shining as usual, Ray wanted to enter the Palace and visit some of the temples from inside. His plan next was to go to Sihanoukville, it made a good mix to alternate between bustling cities and towns and the relaxation of beach towns. The palace was grand and kept in immaculate condition. A group of saffron-clad monks were also visiting to pay their homage and Ray got talking to a group of them. They were boys who were in apprentice in order to practice for a few years, he understood from one of them. There was quite some variety in their characters, the one talking to him had a mischievous look in his eyes and talked with a sparkle of wit. Another one was quite curious whether Ray was a Buddhist and asked, "Have you been a monk too?" evidently curious due to Ray's shaved head.

"No, I think I have sinned too much to be a monk," Ray replied with a smile.

"Yes, but you can become a monk even if you have sinned."

"Really?"

"Yes, you have to live in austerity and beg for food and are true to God for some years."

". . . and what happens if it doesn't work out."

"Then you go back to world."

"As simple as that?" said Ray while thinking that this was quite novel and not how different he had viewed Monks while growing up in India.

"Yes."

"I would like to have a photo with you all, is that ok?"

"Of course."

Little monks in Phnom Phen

Ray reflected on how he used to view Monks as being a homogenous group while he realized that of course each one was an individual with their own ways of connecting with God.

For dinner, he went to a roadside stall, as he had done in every country during backpacking. This one was serving fried chicken; he was the only foreigner in the midst and exchanged smiles all-around. The fried chicken later, he called in for the night and decided to head off to Sihanouksville the next day for some quality beach-time. He looked forward to catching up with Maria, with whom he got on very well. The next morning, he had one last look at 'boom-boom Boulevard', smiled and took a tuk-tuk to the bus-station and bid farewell to this city of extreme contrast.

The inter-city roads were worse than in the previous countries and a bumpy four hour ride later, Ray found himself in Sihanouksville. Maria had written the name of the hotel she had a room at; it was apparently a stones-throw from Serendipity beach. A Rickety tuk-tuk took Ray to the hotel and he could smell the lovely sea-breeze already. His stomach though was growling a bit and he felt a bit uneasy.

Maria was waiting at the hotel when he arrived and a brief inspection later, Ray took a room.

"So, how've you been?" he asked Maria.

"Excellent, went through the mountains from Hoi An to Saigon, then with the boat to Phnom Phen and then here."

"How cool, I also crossed the border on the Mekong!"

"Good to see you again! It's quite a relaxed place here; I've been here for a few days."

"So, any recommendations?"

"Watch the sunset from Serendipity and have an all you can eat BBQ for three dollars."

"Wow, sounds excellent, though my stomach seems to be a bit rough . . . I think from the chicken in the roadside yesterday."

"Oops . . . I was thinking on going to Bamboo Island tomorrow. It's supposed to be very nice, like a deserted Island and you can sleep in a bungalow."

"Did you book already?"

"Nope, but it's quite easy to arrange here. Come on, let's hit the beach."

Ray changed into beach gear and they went to the sands and ordered the all you can eat BBQ. It was probably not such a good idea, as the Sun started going down, so did Ray's stomach and with it, his countenance. Maria knew by this time quite a few of the backpackers around and started making arrangements for Bamboo Island.

"You ok?" she said looking at Ray's face which was getting paler.

"Umm, I think I need to go back to the hotel."

"Will you join us tomorrow to the Island? We need to leave quite early in the morning."

"I don't think so, you go ahead . . . I really need to go now," said Ray as he hurried back to the hotel. Luckily it was just a block away.

It was a bad case of diarrhoea and Ray also felt a fever coming up, it was probably an infection. He took an emergency antibiotic he was carrying from home and took to bed. It got worse in the night, both the stomach cramps and the fever. Ray groaned trying to sleep, but the shivering kept him deliriously awake. It was no better in the morning and Ray resigned himself to recuperating for a couple of days. He mixed an ORS packet with water, drowned half the bottle, took a paracetamol, the next anti-biotic pill in the course and went to sleep. This time around when he woke up, he felt slightly better so made his way outside the hotel room. There was no sign of Maria and her room was empty, so Ray presumed she had gone to the Island. He went out and sat on a bench in the front lawn of the hotel. The Sun was bright and Ray was feeling hot, though perhaps it was due to the fever still inside him.

A kindly looking lady joined him. She seemed Cambodian though was fairer than most of the locals.

"Not going to the beach?" she enquired.

"No, I am quite sick," he said rubbing his stomach to indicate it's diluted state.

"Oh, let me get you something. It is very good."

"Do you mean Loperamide? I am afraid I don't take it, all it does is stop the flow, not cure the actual cause."

"No no, I have a powder which cleans the stomach. It is a natural material and very good. I also sometime get diarrhoea when I come here, I am not used to it anymore. I live in France now."

She went back to her room and fetched a couple of sachets and handed them to Ray along with a glass of water.

"You must mix this in the water. It does not dissolve so you have to drink it quickly and it will clear your stomach along with the germs."

"You French like your medicines eh?" Ray smiled feebly as he examined the sachet. It was a natural compound called Diosmectite and Ray decided to have faith in it.

"Were you born here?" he asked after he had downed the mixture. He almost immediately felt more talkative, perhaps it was placebo effect or that of having someone to tend to him in the absence of friends or family.

"Yes, my parents immigrated to France when I was around ten and now I am married with a Frenchman and have my children grown up there."

"But you feel Cambodian inside?"

"Everybody asks that question! I guess I am a bit of both. I have lived longer in France than here, but I had my first years here. I try to come back on vacations, but it has become less frequent now. My children also travel separate and my husband has to work this time, so I am visiting family. What about you?"

"Well, I was born and brought in India. When I was young, we moved a lot in India as my father was in the Air Force, so we experienced a lot of station-life. It was quite nice actually, living in large bungalows and going to Air-force schools. Then we settled in Delhi where I completed school and university and after working for a couple of years in Delhi I went to the Netherlands where I live in a lovely city called Utrecht."

"Which is your favourite place?"

Ray was hit with the realization that he had lived almost as long in Utrecht as he had in Delhi.

"Well, I feel attached to both cities, in a strange love-hate way, feeling at home when I am there but also longing to be away on vacations. Actually Paris is also one of my favourite cities. I always feel happy when I am walking on Champs Elysees or in the parks and boulevards there, or going to Sacre-Coeur or getting into a cosy Parisian restaurant."

"Funny you say that, I quite like Amsterdam."

"You have to excuse me, I need to visit the restroom," said Ray as he suddenly felt the pressure coming back. He shot into his room, just in time.

When he came back, the lady had bought some bananas. "Have bananas; they also help to solidify your motions."

"That's what my mother taught me too. Thank you so much, you are very kind."

"I think I will have some sleep now. I am meeting my family in the evening for a big dinner."

Ray wondered why she was not staying with the family, but considered that that probably gave more freedom and fewer obligations. He was grateful for the gentle kindness of strangers, that's how God moves in mysterious he thought. He too went back to rest.

In the evening, he was feeling somewhat better and thought that a massage would be good for his aches. He went to a massage place; beach towns were evidently full of these.

The masseuse, on touching him, said, "You sick?"

"Yes, is my body still warm?"

"I have special oil; wait, I get."

The kindness of the masseur gave an inner sense of calm to Ray, which was followed by the cracking of the Kymer massage. Overall, he felt calm and this night he slept well. A good sleep always does wonders and in addition the pills, the mixtures but above all the warmth of people made Ray feel much better the next day. He spent the day at the beach, basking in the Sun and recuperating and was additionally rewarded with the most exquisite sun-set of the entire trip. The Sun went down on the water and against the background of the looming surrounding cliff and boats anchored around.

Sunset at Sihanoukville

"Hey Ray!"

He looked around to see Maria coming over with some other backpackers.

"Hey, had a good trip?"

"Yeah, it was amazing, totally deserted island; we did not even have electricity there. At night, the sea lit up with I think Plankton fish," she said while walking up to him, then paused and added, "Hey, you look quite haggard."

"I've been ill."

"Oh poor you! But you made it to the beach, so a bit better now?"

"Yes, I'll be fighting fit by tomorrow," he said with a smile.

"We're going diving for a couple of days, what do you plan to do?"

"I think I'll head up to Siem Reap once I am feeling ok, am really eager to see the temples of Angkor."

"Sounds like a plan."

The next day he was indeed better. He met the kind Cambodian French lady again in the front lawn and thanked her profusely for helping him.

"You have a kind face; I think people always help you," she said.

That was one of the best compliments Ray had ever received. He gave her some fresh flowers bought from the local market which in turn made her quite happy. Then he went to the massage place, the girl who had helped him the other day was not there, but he left another big tip and told the on-duty staff to give it to her.

Then he went to the beach, to laze around with Maria and her friends. They all lay on easy beach chairs, sipping cocktail mixes of local alcohol and freshly pressed juice.

"You want one too?" said Maria looking up inquiringly.

"Nah, just took antibiotics pills, luckily the last of the course, I'll pass for today."

"We're leaving later for some serious diving around the Islands."

"I think I'll leave tonight or tomorrow for Siem Reap."

"Direct?"

"Yup direct, I had originally wanted to take the boat-trip from Battambang to Siem Reap along the Great Lake."

"The great lake?"

"Yes, I read that the lake was one of the principal reasons for the flourishing of the Khmer empire, the lake water would flow to the sea during the wet season and during the dry season the level would ebb down and water would flow from the sea into the lake. This strange phenomenon led to very fertile grounds for agriculture and abundant fish."

"Wow, so why are you not going by boat?"

"Well, I had a very long boat ride from Vietnam to here and I read that now in the dry season, parts of the river dry up, so you have to take part-boat, part-road transfer. Sounds pretty complicated and I am just recovering from an illness, so I'll spend more time in Siem Reap exploring the temples of Angkor."

"And after that . . . ?"

". . . after that it's the end of this leg of my sabbatical. Am going to visit my parents in Delhi before heading back home to Utrecht, I need to fill in my tax papers et al. Thereafter I'll head to South America or the Caribbean."

"Wow, great plans!"

"What about you?"

"After my diving here, I might go to Siem Reap too, but briefly as I have to get back home to Hungary too. All good things come to an end."

"And are the start of new things," said Ray smiling.

Ray pulled up a beach-chair and stretched himself in the Sun.

After a couple of hours, it was time to part.

"Well, it was a pleasure meeting you," he said to Maria.

"The pleasure was mine."

Ray was still feeling a bit weak from the illness and the antibiotics, so decided to leave in the morning instead of the travails of a night bus. He lingered that day on the beach, and left after the breathtaking Sunset and a light dinner. He called in early for he expected a long day with the bus-service. In any case he would not be in cramped night-bus sleepers.

The day-time bus was however not much of a relief either. The 'direct' service involved a stop-over and a change at Phnom Phen. It was however an eventful stop-over as he met Dutch guy from Utrecht he knew from the Salsa dance. He had travelled from Thailand to Siem Reap and the temples and was going in the opposite direction.

"Small world eh?" said Ray

"I know! I have a theory that people like us will be meeting each other in far-away places very often."

"Eh?"

"Well, people like us love to travel. So the chances that that we travel 'together' to the same far-away destination is high."

"Like a mass migration."

"Something like that."

"Interesting theory. Let's have a drink in Utrecht when we're back."

Soon, Ray was on a bumpy ride to Siem Reap.

The end of the first leg

It was a day-time bus, so the seats were upright instead of a sleeper construction. Sitting next to him was a French girl, Alexandra, a brunette with a je-ne-sais-quoi ambience and quite pleasant company. She was carrying a big camera and dressed in black T-shirt and rugged jeans, which made for a classy backpacker appearance. Ray pondered how the French managed to look stylish even when going to the supermarket.

The bus arrived four hours later in Siem Reap than the indicated time and it was already dark when they reached. Alexandra had ordered a pick-up service from her hotel, so there was someone waiting for her, and she parted. Luckily for Ray there were also tuk-tuk drivers waiting and he found a friendly one who offered to show Ray around a few accommodations. The first one seemed a bit seedy and with the memory of Boom-boom Boulevard still fresh on his mind, Ray decided to look further. The second one was partly under construction, with a new wing in the process of being built, but the already existing one seemed clean and spacious and the owner offered a good price for a double room so Ray took it.

Then the unexpected happened, the tuk-tuk driver did not want any money for his services, instead his deal was to take Ray for a tour of the temples. Business was probably tough this year due to the floods in neighbouring regions; Ray thought for a moment and then accepted the offer.

He refreshed himself, changed and went out for dinner and was quite surprised at this charming French-like town. He had expected it to be very modern in order to cater to the influx of tourists; instead it was quite cute with scattered small-rise houses, there was even a little stream and small bridges linking the opposite sides on the town. The other side of the bridge was however teaming with tourists and eateries were a plenty, starting from roadside stalls featuring one dollar menus.

Ray took the safe course and went into a proper restaurant; it was just a couple of dollars more. Siem Reap was geographically closer to Thailand and Ray could smell the curry flavours emanating from the kitchen, it gave him quite an appetite. That was a good sign that he had completely recovered from his stomach ailment. He ordered a beef stir-fry and a jug of beer to wash it down with.

Meal in Siem Reap

Siem Reap was some eight kilometres away from the temples and since Ray had now some extra time on his hands before departing Cambodia, he decided to take a seven day-pass. He also bought a book, Ancient Angkor, complete with pictures and stories intending to explore the temples at leisure. This was the last travel-stop in his first leg of South-East Asia, before visiting his parents in Delhi and returning home to Utrecht briefly before continuing further on his journey. He did some further reading into the history of Angkor before retiring to bed.

The next morning, there was a tuk-tuk waiting at the hotel, but the driver was the brother of the one who had helped Ray the previous night. The brother did not speak much English, so Ray now understood the deal his brother had made, it was to ensure that the family got enough business. It was such a difference, this collective society to the individualistic ones in the West.

"What's your name?" he asked.

"Arjun"

Ray smiled; it was the name of a character from the Indian epic Mahabharata.

"Grand circuit today ok?" Arjun asked while indicating to Ray on a map.

The temple access had been divided into a grand and mini circuit route. The mini one was the more popular with tourists, especially those for a short stay or on a one-day trip. It seemed that the one-day trippers would fly in, see the sunrise very early at Angkor Wat, see some temples at a swirling pace and thereafter head to the next destination at the end of the day. Not that he had ever done such a whirlwind tour of a country, but especially after this trip, Ray could not imagine taking such a 'vacation'.

"Ok," Ray replied.

The grand circuit covered temples slightly further away from Siem Reap. The first stop was Ta Prohm, which was a large temple monastery complex. Its original name was Rajavihara or the royal monastery, Ray read in the book. Arjun dropped him off on one entrance and with an indication of sign-language and occasional comprehensible English words told Ray that he would wait with the tuk-tuk on the opposite exit.

It was a huge complex, and as he entered the gates, Ray was conscious of a romantic atmosphere provided by the intertwined trees which had grown into the buildings; their massive trunks and roots supporting the structures. This temple had apparently been decided to be left in as close to the state the French had found it in. There was an Indiana Jones feeling to it as nature had taken over the man-made creations.

Indiana Jones feeling

Ray tepidly walked around the ruins, there was a balance betweens the roots of the massive trees holding the structures in place and he did not wish to disturb the equilibrium.

As he gazed into one hallway, half blocked due to the surrounding vegetation and general state of decline, he saw a girl approaching. Ray for a moment thought that he was hallucinating; for she seemed like Daphne coming out of a dream

Daphne re-emerges

"Aye Ray!" she said.

It was no dream!

"Daphne!" he exclaimed, it seemed that he had waited for this moment for eternity without even realizing it. They ran towards each other in Bollywood movie style and hugged whereupon he lifted her and made a small circle in the air. If a filmmaker had been watching, he would have probably shot this in slow-motion and thrown in an odd song in the background.

"Wow, good to see you," he blurted after the euphoria of seeing her had somewhat subsided.

"Look at you, you've changed."

"In what way?"

"When we met, you were this yuppie traveller and now you look like a seasoned backpacker."

"Really, that much difference?"

"Man, you've really tanned too. I could eat you, brownie."

"Umm, perhaps . . ."

"Still the shy-guy I see. You know I hated back then to say goodbye to you but I needed to."

"I understood that . . . and this time?"

"Well, I got your message that you were in Cambodia and also came this way. I was anyways planning to come but now I hurried over. I wrote to you, you didn't write back though?"

"Oh dear . . . I was felled by a stomach flu the past days, didn't really venture into an Internet café."

"Let's enjoy the time we have together ok? I am going to be here for some days."

"So am I, just arrived yesterday."

"So, tell me, where all have you been to?"

"Well, after we parted I went to North Thailand, then to the Islands in South Thailand on the West coast, umm spent Christmas there," Ray blushed a bit thinking of Hilary.

"You should have come to the East coast in Ko Samui; I was there all this time."

"Really?"

"Yeah, first I went to yoga and health Spa, where I detoxified myself, oh my God, I had fresh juices all day, some were yummy, some were horrible."

"You seem to have slimmed down somewhat," said Ray with a wink.

She hit him playfully and continued, "I met a lot of people and partied every night, then I went to a Thai Boxing training school due to which I have now got this kick-ass six-pack," she said leading his hand to her tight tummy.

"I have to be careful not to aggravate you."

"Man, you still use posh-English, that hasn't changed much. Anyways back to you, what did you do next?"

"Went to Kanchanaburi and the Tiger Temple, then flew to Hanoi in Vietnam. Went along the coast by road to South Vietnam, crossed to Cambodia with the Mekong and here I am."

"Did you meet any girls?"

"Lots of them," Ray replied with a wink, which evoked another punch.

"You know what I mean!"

"Well, I did meet someone in Phuket."

"You see! The Islands are so romantic . . ."

There was a pause as Daphne looked away sheepishly.

"Ah, you met someone too!" said Ray, dawning to the conclusion.

"Well, it was a local guy, but he got very possessive. Asian guys want to get married," she said with a laugh.

"Uhh, I am Asian."

"Are you possessive?"

"Why aren't we married yet honey?"

So the banter continued. Suddenly Ray realized that his tuk-tuk was waiting on the other side.

"Amai, Arjun's waiting."

"What, who?"

"My driver."

She tossed back her head while she laughed "Mine too. Shall we head to them?"

"So where are you staying tonight?"

"Umm . . . with you?" she said with a mischievous twinkle in her eye.

"Umm, sure, I have a huge double-room."

"Well, I am at a dorm, so I could check out."

They reached the exit of the temple complex and their respective drivers.

"I'll race you to the next destination," she said as she jumped into her tuk-tuk and said "Go-go," in a style reminiscent of a cowboy egging his horse.

"Do you even know where we are heading?" said Ray laughing.

"Well I am guessing you're also doing the Grand circuit and the routes are the same . . . so eat dust!"

Daphne's temperamental nature was just the perfect compliment to the emotionally steady Ray. The next stop was the magnificent city ruin of Angkor Thom, one of the largest Khmer cities built, covering some nine square kilometres. At the height of the Khmer civilization, it housed about a million inhabitants according to Ray's guidebook. The city was walled and one of the entrance gates was lined with statues leading up to the arched-gate. After passing the gate, they got out of their vehicles to inspect the view from inside the ancient city. Nearby was the Bayon, state temple of the Jayavarman VII and according to the guide one of the most enigmatic religious structures in the world. That had to do with the fact that this structure was the principal temple of successive Kings, who due to the well-guarded Angkor Thom, chose to keep the temple and redesign it, rather than create a new one in a new location.

There was no wall around the structure, Daphne and Ray entered the complex from opposite ends and met in the middle for a quick kiss. After exploring the Bayon with the guidance of the book they thereafter passed the Elephant and Leper-King terraces which probably functioned as terraces for processions. Standing on them, Ray could imagine the pomp and grandeur of the Devarajas watching the crowds and processions go by.

Next they went to the adjoining palace, which was however in a state of derelict. There was a steep step of stairs leading to the top and without hesitation Ray almost ran to the top; perhaps it was the exhilaration of meeting Daphne again or perhaps it was due to his increased condition after months of backpacking; or a combination of both, but he reached the top without stopping. Daphne clapped when he had reached the top.

She joined him and together they sat on the top in the early afternoon Sun and gazed with benevolence at the world below while holding hands.

"I am famished, shall we have lunch soon?" she said eventually.

"I second the motion."

They exited the Angkor Thom complex, indicated to their drivers that they wanted to eat and were taken to a lunch gathering place; which was replete with tents selling food, clothes and souvenirs. It was a welcome break from the heat in the shadow of the eatery. A little girl walked up to them, she was selling postcards. She said, "Ten cards for one dollar, one, two, three, four, five, six, seven, eight, nine, ten," and then proceeded to repeat the counting in French and German. She was so adorable that both Daphne and Ray bought cards off her mother.

"Tough life here eh?" said Ray.

"Yes, did you see the handicapped men here, quite a few of them who lost their limbs when they accidentally stepped on mines laid by the Khmer rouge."

"Yes, so terrible what humans are capable of."

"I know . . . when I was in Ko Samui, I did a lot of meditation . . ."

"Did you get some insights?" asked Ray.

"Have you never meditated?"

"Umm, not really."

"You are pretty non-spiritual for a Hindu, you know!"

"Ah, I dunno, I think there's a certain image of Hindu's and Indians in the west, which periodically gets a new view with some blockbuster movie like Slumdog Millionaire. What is spirituality for me, being kind, doing the right thing, being just. Well, having said that thought perhaps I should give meditation a try. But back to you, what insight did you get?"

"Well, all sorts of thoughts crossed my mind. I tried to make it blank and then suddenly I thought of what I am looking for, why I am travelling and things like that."

"So why indeed?"

"Well, I got my first boyfriend when I was quite young when we both started at University. Then he went to do his PhD in the US and then started working there so the last few years was long-distance. Anyways, we broke up some months back after being about ten years together. So I am enjoying single life now and want to see the world and travel."

"So you don't want to get attached?"

"Nah silly; I am already attached to you. I just don't want to settle. But I think you do, that's why I had to leave you back in Bangkok."

"Lots of assumptions there . . . I want to settle eventually yes, but I am also not certain of what I want to do and where I want to live. You know, when I was twenty I did not what to do with the rest of my life and now I am approaching forty and I still don't know."

"Rest of life sounds so long honey. Funny though; you came across as a very confident yuppie the first time around. Now you seem more uncertain."

Ray smiled and said, "Well, funny that you perceive it so. The yuppie part was perhaps just a façade and maybe on the contrary I am more confident now being myself."

"That's good to know. So what are your plans?"

"I don't really have a clear-cut plan. I think over the years I've got used to this uncertainty principle, now I am sort of comfortable with it. Sometimes I want to chuck it all, the corporate career and instead just be an artist, write a book, paint and be a photographer. But then I think perhaps it's not a good idea to turn a hobby into work . . . Also in order to afford the same lifestyle, I'll need to put in a lot of work in the hobbies then. Plus I think that I'd get bored eventually leading an artist's life, as I also need some intellectual challenge at work."

"You do seem more vulnerable now than before, which is nice."

"Hah, probably again my façade initially, I am really a private person so it takes some time before I open up to someone."

"I am flattered that you open up to me . . . tell me, why did you not come after me to the Islands?"

"Really? Were you expecting me to follow you when you left me? You like someone to chase you?"

"Umm, I guess. I fought a lot for my last relationship but it was one-sided. In the end I gave up. I guess I am looking someone to fight for me."

"I am willing to fight, but it has to come both ways . . . you gave me the vibes that you didn't want to be followed, so I did not."

"Men, you never understand anything!"

"Especially me. Actually I can read non-verbal's very well when it comes to other persons. When it involves me and a girl, it's a catastrophe."

"I think though our tuk-tuk drivers are getting restless. Let's go see some more ruins."

They spend the rest of the day going from one ruin to another, some in a better state than the others. The last stop was one of the most impressive images for Ray, that of Srah Srang meaning Royal Bath, which was a water reservoir and still held it after some nice centuries of creation. It also offered a serene view and the couple watched the Sun go down together.

"Let's go see the sunrise at Angkor Wat tomorrow," said Daphne.

"Oef, we have to wake up really early then and it's supposed to be crawling with tourists."

"Lazy man, let's do it and thereafter we'll go back and sleep all day."

"In any case stay in bed," said Ray with a wink and was prompted poked in the ribs. "Ou, it's beginning to hurt, I think the infatuation is wearing off."

"Ok, ok, I'll stop."

They headed back to Siem Reap town, collected Daphne's backpack et al from the dorm and moved into Ray's hotel-room.

"Wow, quite lux," said Daphne as they entered the room.

Siem Reap room

"It's within my budget of ten euro's per night for a room and except for Bangkok I've been able to stay in a hotel all the while."

"I've stayed in dorms for half the price."

"Well, I am getting a bit old for dorms, I like a good night's sleep plus anyways met a lot of people otherwise, in busses & beaches, restaurants & ruins."

"I sleep like a baby, noise or light doesn't really wake me up."

"That's good news, 'cos I snore."

She once again gave him a little punch and then immediately said, "Oh sorry, I promised not to eh. Old habits die hard."

"So, you hit your boyfriends away?"

"NO! By the way, did you just imply that we were boyfriend and girlfriend?" she asked in an accusing tone.

"Umm, no."

"What no? Aren't we a couple then?"

"Umm, sort of right?"

She laughed. "I love teasing you silly!"

✦

Night-time in Siem Reap was bustling as usual. Daphne coaxed Ray into trying a fancy BBQ restaurant, which would serve a combination of meats, including crocodile and snake.

"Eeeuw," he shivered at the idea.

"We should try some, it probably all tastes like chicken."

"I dare say not. Just the thought of the slimy reptiles."

"Know what, I'll instruct the waiter to say which is which meat only to me."

"Uhhh ok. Afterward we'll have some decadent chocolate ice-cream; I saw this very hip place yesterday. It's also air-conditioned."

They were escorted to a table. There was an "Apsara" (Meaning celestial maiden or celestial nymph) dance show before the food arrived. The BBQ stove-grill was placed between them and true to word, the waitress whispered in Daphne's ear which meat was what. They put a sample of each sort on the grill and after they were cooked, Ray took the first piece. It looked like chicken and tasted like chicken so he moved to the next. Daphne was watching him curiously while eating in her own order. The second piece was actually quite delicious and Ray asked, "Snake?"

"Will tell you later."

Most of the pieces were actually quite good, except one which was rather chewy. That turned out to be the snake, whereas the earlier sumptuous one had been crocodile meat.

"It was good," said Ray approvingly.

"You see, you should always try."

"Well, there are limits. But this was worth a try."

After dinner, they had ice-cream; Ray had a dark chocolate and mango scoops while Daphne had Lychee and banana scoops. It was a steeply priced joint by Cambodian standards, but the air-conditioning was quite welcome in the warm and humid climate.

They walked back hand-in hand to the hotel and a couple of hours later . . . were in dream-land. The next morning, Arjun came to pick them up at four in the morning in order to catch the sun-rise.

"You slept well?" asked Ray who had not quite slept owing to a combination of too much food and someone sleeping next to him.

"Like a baby."

And so they went to Angkor Wat. The road towards it was already busy with tuk-tuks and tourist-busses. When they reached they had to pass through controls which took a while due to the great number of tourists lining up. Angkor Wat, meaning Temple City, was the world largest religious monument; it housed a complete realization of the Hindu mythology of Mount Menu in the centre of the complex. It was originally dedicated to Ray's favourite Hindu God Vishnu though was later converted into a Buddhist temple. It was too dark to see, but they could sense the grandeur of the place and Ray whispered, "We'll come back to see it in more detail ok?"

Once in, they followed the mass of people to a moat of water from which they could dimly see the main tower in the distance. This was supposedly the best place to see the Sun rise from behind the tower and reflect on the water. The hour came, but the sky was quite misty so the Sun rise was a bit of a disappointment. Someone in the crowd said in an exasperated tone, "Was this it?"

"Well, since we are here anyway, let's see a bit more of the main complex, shall we? It's influenced by the Dravidian architecture from the South of India. Angkor Wat was still in use by the locals as a worship place all the while," suggested Ray.

"Sure."

A climb of stair brought them to the first level. The crowds had thinned out by then, most of them probably to the next tick-in-the-box sight.

"Hey look, the Sun's coming out," observed Daphne suddenly.

"Let's get back to the water; I think we'll still get a lovely view."

They rushed back to the moat and indeed, the Sun was still in the early morning hues and warmth of the rays cleared the mist somewhat. There were now only a handful of people around the water and they had a very romantic view of the sun slowly rising above the silhouette of the tower and splashing its glorious colours in the sky and on the water. Ray put his arms around Daphne and they snuggled.

"Well, I am done for today," he said at last.

"Ok sleepy head, let's go back for some sleep and we could do some shopping later."

"Great plan; this is my last stop before getting back to the normal world, so I can do some serious shopping."

"I'll have to ship it back to my parents."

Ray appreciated that she did not ask him to carry stuff back. As a principle he did not carry other people's stuff, no matter how close they were. In this case though, he would have had a tough time saying no.

A beauty sleep later, they headed toward the shops. On the way though, one of those incidents occurred which brought a tear to Ray. In a small shop, there was a man teaching English to small (street) children. It was the weekend and they understood that this man always taught every weekend, to give these children a better opportunity to succeed in life. The man did not accept any donations, instead he asked Ray to teach some English to the class. Ray gladly took the chance, the agenda was the English alphabet elucidated with the use of examples and soon the little shop was reverberating to 'A for apple, B for ball and so on . . .' Daphne clapped.

The interlude later, they made their way to the shops. Ray bought a crocodile leather belt and wallet and diverse oils with the Lavender flavour, his favourite natural scent. Daphne bought diverse silk objects, table-clothes, shawls and earrings. She arranged for the items to be shipped. She seemed quite adept at arranging things.

"Let's rent cycles tomorrow and go to the less visited sites," she exclaimed suddenly whilst passing a bike-rent store. The Dutch and their love for bikes was always apparent. So they did and the next morning was a lovely day, not too warm and a bit cloudy, so the Sun did not bear down that hard. They cycled under the trees and gentle breeze; there were few tourists around, even fewer vendors and all was bliss.

They explored the bas reliefs of Angkor Wat, engraved on the walls were stories from Indian mythology, from the tales of Mahabharat and Ramayana which Ray explained with great detail to Daphne who listened with attention.

"Wow, amazing that you know all these stories."

"My mother used to tell me these stories as a child. Plus of course I did some refreshing through the book I bought."

"You're so different from the other guys."

"Thanks, I take that as a compliment," he winked.

"Where are we heading though? I am going East and you're going back West."

"Do you want to settle down after all?" Ray smiled gently and put his arms around Daphne's shoulder

"No, I was wondering what it would be like if you came travelling with me."

"It would be great; however I would like to see my parents for my birthday in March. My mother is quite looking forward to the home-coming. Then I also need to fill my tax return before the end of March and also talk to my boss whether my position is still secure before I continue further on my sabbatical."

"Commercial man . . . Take a risk!"

"Well, I have taken a big risk to take half a year off during the crisis. I mean, I am not asking you to come back with me either eh?

I just need to do these things . . . but afterwards, THIS time I will come after you. I still have almost four months to go."

"Really? I am going to Australia next."

"Umm, I've been there already . . . Where to afterwards?"

"South America!"

"I've always wanted to go to Peru, Machu-Pichu has been long on my list. Or Cuba? Or some such combination?"

"That could work! I think I'll be in Oz for a month or so and then head to South America."

"You have a year off right?"

"Well, I have off till my money lasts."

"In which case, keep it short in Oz, heard it's become really expensive since I was there."

"Well, a couple of weeks in any case . . ."

"And thereafter we meet in Peru!"

"Yes!"

"As a couple?"

"You prefer travelling alone?"

"Umm, I think that's nice as the next best choice. The nicest is to travel with your lover."

"Correct answer."

"And thereafter?"

"We see. You'll go back to your job I suppose."

"If my position is still there yes, one of us needs some stability eh?"

"Well yeah, but I still need to see the world."

"So you should, we'll see as it goes ok?"

"Ok."

He kissed her thankfully as the Sun went down slowly.

✦

The next days passed quickly as they explored the temple-complexes of Angkor and the more far flung ruins like Rollos; the sigh-seeing alternating with hanging around Siem Reap and having conversations on every topic under the Sun.

The reasons of the decline of the kingdom were multi-fold, the newer kingdoms of Cham and Siem were better positioned for trade and thereafter the Angkor kingdoms were sacked repeatedly by the Kings of Ayutthaya (later day Siem /Thailand). In the end, the empire came to an end and left the world with this great heritage.

The departure day came; Ray was flying westwards to Delhi, India to see his parents. Daphne was taking the bus later in the day to head eastwards. She came with Ray to the airport to see him off. This parting was surprising easy-going, perhaps due to the fact that they were planning to meet up soon.

"Stay other from other women."

"I think you have more chances with mingling than I do."

"Well, see you in a couple of weeks."

"Yeah, I'll check for flights to Lima."

Ray's back-pack was almost twenty kilos now, a far cry from the initial thirteen he had started with; it had gradually filled up with souvenirs and clothes. This would be one of his advices to any starting backpacker, to travel light and only to carry the bare essentials.

On the flight, he thought about the things he had learnt on this sabbatical. One thing which stood out was the big-family feeling of backpacking travellers in general. It was so easy to have contact with others; perhaps travelling alone enhanced that ability. There was camaraderie, respect and helpfulness from total strangers who were best friends for days, only to part a couple of days later.

The amazing experiences, breathtaking sceneries and awe-inspiring creations on the one hand and the at-times loneliness were all part of the journey. The brilliance of amazing local cuisines and flavours made for a contrast to the occasional stomach flu's and ailments.

Ray had not thought about how easy or difficult it would be, but in the end it was surprisingly easy to travel. There were twenty year olds travelling the world, so he wondered why people fussed so much or planned for so long.

The friendliness of the backpackers was more than matched by the open-heartedness and generosity of the locals. Most people in the world had a good heart, barring the small minority who were in for a quick rip-off. What was even more heart warming was that the seemingly poor people were happy with what they had and had the aspiration to achieve more with their hard work.

Though he was a bit sad at ending the first leg of his sabbatical, he was also looking forward to getting home, first to his parents and then to Utrecht. On a personal level, although he had started out without any ambition to 'find himself' or the like, he realized that now he had somewhat focused on what he liked and wanted from life. His main purpose was to be happy and Ray was happy in dabbling in the arts like painting, photography, dancing and being free in general but at the same time having some intellectual challenge at work. He also came to the conclusion that he liked his life in Utrecht; it afforded him the precious work-life balance.

He also liked to finish what he started and he was relishing the thought of writing a book.

'Everybody had a novel in them, so why not me?' he thought as they landed in Delhi.

All this made his happy and that feeling was compounded tenfold as he was in love, he had fallen for Daphne actually from the moment he had seen her and the past week had been enchanting. She seemed the perfect complement to his ways and he was looking forward to meeting her again in Peru or the Caribbean.

The immigration official gestured with his hand for Ray's passport and landing card and enquired, "Business or pleasure?" as he stamped the entry.

"Pleasure sir," said Ray and passed onwards into the sprawling metropolis.

Author's note

This is a semi-fictional book based on my actual travel to South-East Asia. While travelling I'd kept a blog which was always much appreciated by my friends and even strangers. When I returned home, I had quite a few suggestions to develop a book out of it. I spent a long time vacillating whether to do so and what genre to write.

In the end I chose for fiction and to write a novel rather than a travel-log. I drew upon characters from my travels and experience and tried to paint a light-hearted romantic travel adventure. Needless to say, some characters are fictional and others modified. A special thanks to all who helped me in this endeavour; to Joyce for editing, to my Mother Shampa who reviewed the ending of the book and to Murray and Rashmi who reviewed the beginning.

The photos are real, that is, I made them whilst travelling. Some chapters have fewer photos due to the fact that my USB flash reader got infected by a virus halfway around my travel. I could recover some of them, but others are lost, only imprinted in my memory.

It was great to write this novel, as I could relive my journey all over again! I hope you have as much fun reading it.